Them Shes Be Pirates

The continuing true account of the
adventures of E. Pluribus Van Slyke,
Lt. (jg), Ret., in the taming of the pirate
menace and the securing of American
womanhood.

As recorded by

E. Pluribus Van Slyke

in a world orchestrated by

M.E. Meegs

The Oeuvre of M.E. Meegs

Empyreal Privateer

Virtue at Market Price

Them Shes Be Pirates

No Time for Fish Tales

Hush, My Inner Sleuth

LycophosPress.com

The Byblos Foretold Novaplex

All's Fair, Mrs. Biddle

Babes at Sea

Peddlers All

Dames Engaged

The Fly Maiden's Book of Virtues

The Circensiad

ByblosForetold.com

Them Shes Be Pirates

M.E. Meegs

&

E. Pluribus Van Slyke

Lycophos Press

Northampton, Mass.

First Print Edition 2018

Lycophos Press
Northampton, Mass.

ISBN: 978-1-938710-36-0

For girls gone pirate

CHAPTER 1.

MUTINY OF THE BOUNTY

This being my second outing on a plank that eventful year, I at least had some idea of what to expect: sheer, unmitigated terror. Only this time, it was a good deal worse. On the first occasion, I'd been perched seventy-five feet above the open sea, with my wrists tied, and wearing nothing but a tattered union suit. At present, I was six thousand feet over the rocky shores of Maine, with both wrists *and* ankles tied, and wearing nothing at all. Even the plank was inferior: barely ten inches wide and not one thick.

I believe the dissimilarities in circumstances can be attributed to two things. First, my prior foray had been on the luxury liner S.S. *Paris*, and the cord that bound me was silk. This venture was aboard *Lucy's Revenge*, a run-down airship named for a venereal disease, and it was rough jute digging into my wrists and ankles. Second, my tormentors on that earlier occasion were middle-aged men—undeniably disagreeable, but overweight and slow-moving. This time, they were five of the Mortal Sins—all quite deadly, and all in their prime. And while I'll grant that Sloth didn't put much into the tormenting, her sister Wrath happily took up the slack.

I suppose an opening such as this begs some explanation. If you've read the previous installment, you know that I'd recently rescued Sesbania, the woman I called my wife, from Jean Lafitte's auction block in St. Pierre (the French island just south of Newfoundland). And, a couple nights before that, been wedded to the Muses Clio and Melpomene and their half-sisters Pride, Avarice, Envy, Wrath, and Sloth, in a Mormon ceremony conducted by their father, the mad pirate Captain Bonnet. You also know a good deal else I won't waste time recounting.

If you *haven't* read the previous installment, you really don't have much of a chance at all. Better go pick it up before it falls out of print.

We made our escape immediately after the rescue. The sun had risen by the time we boarded and we made excellent time, as steam-powered airships are wont to do on clear days. After setting us on course for Louisiana and the Lafitte brothers' base at Barataria, I retired to my cabin and napped beside Sesbania until just after noon. When I emerged, Horatio—my executive officer and only crewman who could read a compass—informed me that my wives (Sins and Muses) had arranged to have the gun deck turned into a bathhouse.

I suppose I ought to have seen this coming. You see, along with their trousseaux, the girls had brought aboard a steamfitter named Percival. He was to make improvements to the ship's primitive bathroom facilities. Anticipating that seven wives would make some serious demands on the plumbing, I voiced no objection. Nor did I object when they turned the oar deck into their harem. The oars were meant to power the ship at night, or when clouds occluded the sun. They performed this feat via some mysterious property which had nothing to do with rowing per se, but merely the work going into it.

As it happens, your average Sin puts a great deal of work into bickering, bad-mouthing, and badgering. Place several in close quarters, and you can add backbiting (both figurative and literal) to the list. Why, just setting a plate with an odd number of doughnuts before Avarice and Envy would be enough to create a perpetual-motion machine.

So the oars I considered expendable. The gun deck, however, I felt vital. Apart from a few cutlasses, it held our entire arsenal: a dozen steam cannons. They could shoot a variety of projectiles, but our magazine now held only offal. (Yes, that's right, rotting entrails.) Not quite as effective as a dreadnought's sixteen-inch guns firing high-explosive shells, but I currently resided in a fictional world where high explosive—or even gunpowder— seemed not to exist. And as they say, when in Rome, one must do as the Romans do. (Though whether even fictitious Romans fire offal from steam cannons is a question I can't answer.)

With only this meager weaponry as defense, we sallied forth into a veritable sea of lethal hazards. As I mentioned earlier, we were then on our way to the base of the ruthless Lafittes, pirate brothers whom we'd already quite thoroughly annoyed. What's more, we'd absconded with a good deal of loot belonging to my father-in-law, the quite incontrovertibly insane Captain Bonnet. Lastly, there was my apparent abandonment of the swashbuckling Jack Tigue, a man who made evisceration of the ignoble into something of a hobby. So, three bloodthirsty pirate bands to be reckoned with.

Needless to say, proceeding without our main armament would be utter lunacy. I went up to the gun deck to nip the foolish idea in the bud. And with such determination that I ignored Pride's attempt to distract me with her charms—a matched pair, which she displayed to their full advantage whilst accosting me in the passageway.

I put my foot down, ordered Percival to cease work, and told the girls they'd have to make do without a bathhouse. That was about a minute and thirty seconds prior to where I began my account, out on the plank. When their interests are aligned, Sins work with a startling efficiency. All except Sloth, of course.

Avarice, who had plans to make further use of my resemblance to her brother-in-law and Bonnet's number two—a man named Smedley—suggested some inconspicuous amputation. Envy and Wrath voted with her, with Sloth naturally abstaining. But their proud sister's vanity would not be so easily slaked. When you spurn an offering of Pride's, you do so at your peril. It was she who suggested the plank. Wrath warmed to the idea quickly and, with a little hair-pulling, Sloth made it a majority.

The situation could have been resolved much earlier, but even before stripping me naked and binding my wrists and ankles, the girls had gagged me. They stuck one end of a plank out a gun port and then Avarice, who by that point was caught up in the spirit of the thing, produced the horsewhip she kept ever handy. A few cracks, and I hopped up onto the board. I had to duck to make it through the gun port, which made it doubly difficult, but by then Wrath had taken control of the whip and the lashes were biting my flesh with conviction. I looked back at them entreatingly, but their sole reply was a cascade of cackling. (They *were* half-pirate, after all.)

It wasn't until I was on the very precipice that Pride asked if I wanted to reconsider my decision. I nodded—carefully, given the precariousness of my position, but quite unmistakably. I wasn't entirely sure which decision she meant, re her charms or the bathhouse, but my regret was complete enough to cover all three.

Once they allowed me to hop back in, all seemed forgiven. We even shared a laugh. Well, they shared a laugh. The best I could manage was a weak smile. But I don't want you to get the idea I let them walk all over me. After some tense negotiations, they agreed to open the bathhouse to adult men on alternate Wednesday afternoons.

On my way out, I whispered a suggestive comment to Pride. She looked at me with disgust, then slapped me so hard my head spun. I took that to mean I'd repaired the damage I'd done earlier. It was imperative that *she* do the spurning.

Licking my wounds, I retired to the relative serenity of the control room. But the respite was brief. Soon hideous noises pierced the calm from above. Melpomene had found the calliope. If you remember your mythology, she's the Muse of dramatic tragedy. Her singing lamentations *a cappella* had been bad enough, but the steam-organ accompaniment took the misery to a whole new level. I'd never harbored any illusions about married life, but neither had I imagined anything like this.

I looked in on Sesbania and saw she was still sound asleep in my bunk. Given her recent ordeal, waking up to Melpomene's gloomy cacophony might well prove too much for her fragile condition. Valiantly, I made my way up to the loft that held the malevolent instrument of torture. (Calliopes may be de rigueur in a circus parade, but they really should be banned from all other uses.)

I found the mournful Muse weeping uncontrollably. She was nearly always weeping uncontrollably, but now she combined it with chant-like songs in what I took to be Greek. Mercifully, on seeing me she paused the infelicitous performance. Even the weeping became some-what measured.

"What do you think?" she asked, but fortunately didn't wait for an answer. "I had Percival make some adjustments to facilitate playing the pentatonic scale. I've been working on arrangements to accompany the chorus in *Antigone*. It really brings out the pathos, don't you think?"

"Yes. Almost too well. I'm just afraid Sesbania might not be able to take too much pathos at the moment."

"Oh. Yes, I see. That poor girl! One can hardly imagine what she's been through.... I don't suppose she's shared any details yet?"

"No, and it seemed best not to ask."

"Of course.... But should she later, you wouldn't mind jotting down some notes? We really could use some new plotlines."

"But you don't write the stuff yourself, do you?"

"No, just inspire. Though it's been rather difficult finding prospects lately. I do have one I think might work out. Have you seen any of Eugene O'Neill's plays?"

"Not that I recall."

"I'm testing him out now with the old Phaedra plot—you know, stepmother falls in love with stepson. I think he has potential. An admirably bleak outlook on life.... By the way, Clio stopped by earlier to ask my forgiveness. Said the Sins were giving you a rough time."

"Why would she need your forgiveness?"

"Her destruction of *Titus Andronicus*, of course."

"A favorite of yours?"

"Are you kidding? Betrayal, murder, rape, savage revenge.... What isn't to like? Anyway, I did forgive her.... Poor kid. Father really did use her." She'd been teary-eyed throughout the conversation, but now the flood-gates reopened. "She's so lucky to have escaped to you! ...Of course, *you* may betray her.... Do you think you will? Or me?"

"Betray you how?"

"Oh... Yes. Nothing's happened to betray, has it? No real wedding night... Sad... Not that I'm blaming you.... Your hands are full, aren't they?"

She was looking decidedly forlorn. And, I might add, curiously fetching in the process. That may sound diffi-cult to believe, given her pale complexion and waif-like figure—not to mention the constant sobbing. But unlike with other girls, the weeping somehow became her. Her eyes never became puffy. Instead, the tears gave them a glow. And her lips quivered in a way one could easily interpret as anticipation. Her long dark-brown hair fell straight and looked perpetually damp. Not normally attractive in a woman, but it worked in her case. I sat on the bench beside her and she fell into my arms.

She responded to my every kiss and each caress as if they'd saved her from the very brink of despair. So you can imagine how she regarded my work under the robe. I flatter myself I'm a bit of an expert when it comes to giving a girl's gondolier a workout. But I can honestly say I'd never taken a woman to such heights of ecstasy—and I'm including the episode when I'd given Sesbania a whiff of the aphrodisiacal perfume [Ed. note: see Book One].

Melpomene didn't conjugate Greek, or recite the Athens telephone directory; she just moaned. But that girl knew how to moan. She put body and soul into it. It would start with a quick, uncontrollable shiver, from the toes on up. Then the moan proper began, with a mono-syllabic "Ahh!" followed by a rapid crescendo, which immediately led into a climactic trochee, the first syllable a sustained "Ohhh!" and then the finale, delivered in a higher octave—another "Oh," though this one much shorter, and appreciably quieter. Afterward, the coda: another quick shiver, this one starting at the head and running to the feet.

When I ventured inside, I thought her tremors of delight would kill us both. Either our anatomies were somehow perfectly matched, or this was one very sensuous young lady. Whichever, I felt pleased to have her as a member of the harem.

The moment things were over, she pulled me close, then whispered in my ear, "Go. I know you must...."

"No hurry, really."

"There's no avoiding it! So go now!"

She shoved me away, and immediately took to bawling. I began then to understand her psyche: the lovemaking needed to be perfect so my departure would be all the more tragic.

Well, just so she was happy.

II

I returned to the control room to find Seaman Second Class Albertson at the helm. He was the last member of my crew, in every sense—an ugly and thoroughly brutish gob with the intellect of a mop handle. As long as manning the helm required nothing more than holding steady, he could usually be trusted not to send us descending in a fatal spiral. But not for more than five or ten minutes at a stretch. Apparently, in this case, it had been something more than that.

"I'll take over. Where's Horatio?"

"Button needed mendin', or so Mattie told him. I think it was listenin' to you two up in the organ loft that got her engine runnin'."

"Oh. Ah... Melpomene was scoring the chorus in *Antigone*. That must be what you heard."

"*Somebody* was scorin', all right." He looked over at the door to my cabin, where Sesbania slept, and shook his head.

I'd never have expected to be admonished by a simple salt over an act of infidelity—unless, perhaps, it involved his wife. What made the situation all the more ironic, Sesbania and I were not actually married. Whereas Melpomene and I were. Assuming, that is, you have an open mind when it comes to polygamy.

Albertson, however, was under the impression Sesbania had been my wife since before the present adventure began, mainly because I had told that small lie. But at this precise moment, he'd become distracted by a series of barrels passing by the windows on our port side.

"What's that about?" he asked.

"I suspect Percival is disposing of the offal. I've decided to have him turn the gun deck into a bathhouse."

"Yeah, we heard about you decidin' that." He grinned a nearly toothless grin, then looked down through the canted window. "Who'll be getting' it?"

"I believe we're over New Jersey."

"Serves 'em right...."

The door to my cabin opened and Sesbania looked out at us. She was wearing one of my shirts, but had neglected to button it. Albertson noticed too.

"You'd better get something to eat," I told him.

He was blushing. I hadn't known ordinary seamen were even capable of blushing.

When he'd gone, Sesbania approached and gave me a kiss, then wrapped her arm around mine.

"What was all that noise a while ago?"

"Noise? Oh, just one of the girls practicing. Melpomene, I think it was. You met her last night—the weeper. Muse of tragic poetry during working hours. Anyway, how'd you sleep?"

"Like a log. Thank you for not... Well, for letting me sleep. After all these weeks of celibacy, I bet you're feeling pretty randy, aren't you?" She looked me in the eye now, and, apparently, determined the answer for herself. "Well, even if you weren't *entirely* chaste, I do want you to know those pirates never took advantage...."

"No? That's lucky. Not many pirates would show such restraint."

"I don't think it was restraint so much as indifference. The Lafittes' taste runs... well, elsewhere."

"Elsewhere?"

"Toward other men.... The whole band seemed inclined that way."

"I suppose that explains their talent for close-harmony cackling."

"Does it? If anything, I was lonely most of the time. And until taking me to the auction house, they actually treated me quite well. I had a room with a bath. My meals were left on a tray for me on a table outside the door. Someone would ring a bell, and there it would be. And they had a very good chef. French, of course. Anyway, it wasn't until the day before you arrived that things turned ugly. They stripped me naked, in order to appraise my value on the auction block." She shivered. "But let's not talk about that anymore. Let's just think about the present. Right now, I'm famished."

Horatio had emerged by then and once he took the helm (and I'd buttoned her shirt), I escorted Sesbania to the galley. Dottie was there, as she often was, and had just put out some fresh bread, cheese, and cold meat for Albertson, her consort. He shared it with us, and Sesbania ate heartily. But I was too preoccupied by my thoughts. My mind kept turning to her story of captivity. Certain parts didn't jibe.

When she felt sated, she asked if I'd like to join her for a nap. We went into the cabin together, but it quickly became obvious she meant *nap*. No sooner had she slid under the covers than she fell into a deep sleep. I gave her a peck on the cheek and tiptoed out the door.

"Didn't expect to see you so soon," Horatio said. "I guess it's a good thing you got those spares upstairs. Does the little lady know about them yet?"

"No. I need to think of a way to break it to her."

"In the meantime, the little black girl's been asking for you."

"Clio? Any idea what it's about?"

"She's turning the aft hold into a library, and wants to get your opinion. Least that's what she said. You have a library card?" He chuckled at his little joke. "Well, I don't suppose you need one. But remember: in the library, one's gotta be quiet."

I left him chuckling and climbed up to the hold. There I found the Muse of history unpacking cases of the faux champagne her father had duped me with. Once they'd been emptied, she stacked the wooden crates on their sides as makeshift shelves. So far, she had a hundred feet of shelving and five of books.

Bonnet had given me the champagne as part of the girls' collective dowry. But when I refer to him as Clio's father, I'm using the term loosely. Clio was as dark-skinned as her sister Melpomene was light. I'd met their mother, Mnemosyne, and she fell somewhere in be-tween—a Saracen perhaps. Clio, however, most definitely had African blood. Her eyes were as brown as her com-plexion, her lips full, and she wore her hair in beaded braids that emitted a succession of clicks whenever she turned her head quickly. And though somewhat short, the sum of her surface area was amplified by her bounti-ful curvature.

"I've plenty of room for expansion," she said, smil-ing at her collection. That was her most winning feature: she alone among the seven sisters was inclined to smile. What's more, it was a smile that exhibited neither scorn or contempt.

"I might have a few volumes to contribute. Depend-ing how discerning you are."

"For now, not too discerning. Horatio told me we would pass near Washington."

"Probably not too far from it right now."

"You know, they have a very big library there."

"Yes, the Library of Congress. Very impressive. You'd like to visit it?"

"Oh, I've visited it before. What I'd like to do now is raid it."

"Raid it?"

"Yes—not take everything, of course. Just a selec-tion. I'm sure I could talk Wrath into coming along. And Pride never wants to be left behind."

"I'm afraid it's not in the cards. They keep a good many soldiers stationed in Washington."

"The British managed to raid it. Burned it to the ground."

"That was quite a long time ago. They aren't so careless these days. Besides, Avarice has her heart set on raiding the Pelican barroom in Barataria, and I more or less committed to it."

She shrugged, but I could tell her disappointment was real.

"I'll tell you what, after Barataria we can take on a small public library or two."

"OK, but let's make it one at a college. They always have a rare book room."

"Do you favor rare books? After your treatment of *Titus Andronicus*, I wondered if you had something against them."

"Oh, no. Just that one in particular. Though I'm afraid I upset Melpomene."

"She told me you apologized."

"So it *was* you I heard with her." She playfully wagged a finger at me.

"Well..."

"It's OK. You're married, aren't you? By the way, how's that first wife of yours getting along?"

"Ah, it's funny you should ask. Just between you and me, I find myself having doubts...."

"You seemed to be working fine with Melpomene." She winked.

"No, I mean doubts about Sesbania. It's her account of her abduction. The details don't fit together quite right."

"What is it you suspect?"

"Well, that she might not be Sesbania, but a double."

"Like you and Smedley?"

"Yes, exactly."

"But if you can't tell your own wife, who can?"

"Well, outwardly she's the same. At least as far as I remember. She's been uncharacteristically agreeable, but that might just be due to exhaustion, and relief at having been rescued. Could easily clear up in a day or so. Anyway, she knew Sesbania's feelings toward facial hair, and about a scar on my leg."

"A scar on your leg? Interesting.... Were you gored by the white tusk of a wild boar?"

"Ah, no. Not exactly. The sharp boot of an angry schoolgirl. Beth, Beth Hastings. Objected when I offered to help her make snow angels. But you don't want to hear that yarn. Anyway, this apparent Sesbania also knew we weren't in fact married."

"You aren't?"

"No—but we were planning to be, eventually. Maybe keep that under your hat for now."

"All right. But can't you just ask her some other questions until you're sure?"

"She claims not to remember much from before her abduction from the steamship."

"Well, it must have been very traumatic."

"Yes, but it's her account of her captivity that really begs credulity. Before leaping to conclusions, I thought maybe I'd consult you. I'm hoping there might be some historical antecedent that could explain things."

"Oh, I see. Go ahead, tell me."

"First, you need to know that she'd been wearing our bankroll, sewn into her chemise. It was in large denominations, to be less conspicuous. But rather obvious when handling said undergarment. Second, there's no sign of the money now and she appears to have no memory of it. Third, last week when I passed through Barataria, one of Lafitte's men mentioned the mole on her bum. Fourth, she claims that it wasn't until just before the auction that any of them saw her naked. Which, while comforting, seems rather un-pirate-like."

"Well, in Shakespeare's *Pericles*, the pirates don't molest Marina."

"And it doesn't strike you as implausible?"

"No more than the rest of that ridiculous play.... But even before the auction, she would have needed to bare her bum to take a pee."

"She claims she had her own room and private bath."

"Those were some *very* hospitable pirates. They sound more like Gilbert and Sullivan than Shakespeare."

"Yes. *If* her story's true. I'd like to give her the benefit of the doubt, but I need some logical explanation in order to believe it. Even if she didn't remember having the money, she would have noticed it. And how did that pirate know about her mole?"

She reached for a book. "Ahh... It's right here, in your beginner's library. *The Decameron,* day two, ninth story. One of Filomena's. A merchant makes a bet he can seduce another man's wife. But in fact, he finds she's too virtuous to sleep with him. So he hides in a chest and has it taken to her chamber. That night he emerges. He takes some proofs of his visit, and notes a mole just beneath the wife's breast—yet forbears to take advantage of her. He returns to the chest and it's removed the next day. Believing he lost the bet, the husband instructs his servant to execute his mistress for her unfaithfulness. Luckily, the retainer is too weak-kneed to go through with it." She now took out the huge volume of Shakespeare. "It's here as well, in *Cymbeline,* the Bard's underappreciated parody of himself and his plays."

"So someone hiding in the room emerges at night, perhaps the very first night, takes her chemise and sees her bum. Then goes back into hiding without waking her. Seems rather involved. Pirates aren't usually so subtle."

"Well, I didn't say it was *likely,* only an antecedent. Just makes a good story. No, I think the pirates had their way with your girl, and she's reluctant to tell you. Or her subconscious is blocking the memory and she really *does* have amnesia. Mother could get to the bottom of that."

"Your mother's a practitioner of Freudian analysis?"

"No, no. The goddess of memory. But we can forget about all that nonsense and get down to why you really came to see me.... I *thought* I must be next on your list."

"Next on my the list?"

"Sloth, Envy, Avarice, Melpomene... I assume you're working up to Wrath and Pride. You'll have your hands full with them."

"Yes—but..."

"Oh, come on. All this twaddle about a mole and a chemise money-bag, and pirates who don't take advantage. In truth, you came to take advantage of *me,* didn't you?"

It honestly hadn't been my intention, but I admit I was quickly warming to the idea.

"You'll have to take a raincheck, I'm afraid," she said. "Auntie Selene is here for a visit."

"Auntie Selene?"

"Cousin, really. Goddess of the moon, lunar cycles... Used euphemistically to refer to catamenia."

"Catamenia?"

"*It's my time of the month.*"

"Oh, of course."

She moved in close and kissed my cheek. "Besides, husband, you *really* need a bath. It must have been very hot up in Melpomene's loft."

She went back to her books, giggling, and I went off to follow through on her advice.

III

It was after seven when I arrived back in the control room.

"I'll take the helm," I told Horatio. "You can go and get something to eat."

"OK, boss. But you might want to keep an eye out for wifie number one."

"What do you mean?"

He pointed with his thumb in the direction of my cabin. "The parrot's been in there talking."

"Wait here a minute."

"Aye, aye, sir." He gave me one of his mock salutes.

I opened the cabin door in time to hear the parrot do a very good imitation of another librarian of my recent acquaintance, one residing in Port Jervis, New York.

"*Nothing exotic,*" he chimed. "*Now let's get to it!*"

I threw a tumbler at it, but missed; the glassware shattered against the wall.

"*Now, how would you like a taste of a real woman?*" he asked rhetorically.

Swinging a cutlass, I chased him out and shut the door. Sesbania was sitting up in bed, laughing.

"Where did he learn all that?"

"Well..."

"I wonder who it was who objected to the exotic?

And just what she was referring to. You should have heard him moaning! Just like Melpomene.... That is her name, isn't it?"

"Yes, that's right."

"There was something downright primal about it, animalistic—and yet... somehow erotic. Was she alone, do you think?"

She wasn't laughing now.

"Maybe it's time we had a chat," I said. "About her and her sisters."

"They're sisters? They certainly don't look like it."

"Well, half-sisters. They're daughters of Captain Bonnet, the mad pirate of Barbados."

"How bizarre. But what are they doing here?"

"It's a complicated story."

"I've time."

"Well, to begin with, I'd amassed a sizable haul of fine liquor by raiding the home of a bootlegger—a shady character named Gatsby. I'd been told that was the currency I'd need to redeem you at auction. But the night before we rescued you, Bonnet waylaid us. He took the liquor, and most of my crew. I was powerless to stop him."

"But you did at least try?"

"I only learned he took the liquor after it was too late. You see, he distracted me by serving a lavish meal, and introducing various of his daughters. Well, after he'd purloined the booze he, or I should say, his son-in-law, offered to give back a large portion of it, *if*..."

"If what?"

"If I married some of the daughters."

"*Some?*"

"Bonnet's a Mormon. With a lot of daughters to unload. Anyway, what could I do? Without the liquor, I couldn't gain your freedom."

"But of course, you *did* free me without it."

"Yes. See, it turned out Bonnet tricked me. Gave me inferior goods. Faux champagne and ersatz Scotch. And instead of two Muses, three Virtues, and two Sins, I wound up with two Muses and *five* Sins! The man's a horrible cheat."

She spent most of a minute trying to digest that, then gave her head a little shake. "But forced marriages aren't binding. Especially ones as ridiculous as these. As long as you haven't consummated..." She stopped mid-sentence and gave me a piercing stare. It was Sesbania, all right. "How many?"

"Just two. Melpomene and Envy." I was glad now that Avarice was too selfish, and Sloth too sleepy, to be added to the list. "Just sort of happened. Anyway, I don't think Bonnet takes returns—or that they'd be willing to go."

"For Christ's sake, Pluribus! Where's that leave me?"

"Oh, first in my affections."

"I damn well better be!"

I sat down and embraced her reassuringly.

"How ironic," she said. "These seven strangers have a claim on you, but not me! Now I insist we get married."

"You don't object to the others?"

"Of course I do! But I suppose I'll just have to adjust. As long as I *am* first in your affections."

"Of course. But for safety's sake, let's not state that so candidly in front of Envy. Or Pride."

She was laughing again, thankfully. "What an absurd situation!"

"Frankly, from the time I entered this make-believe

world, it's been one absurdity after another."

"What do you mean, make-believe world?"

"Oh. That's right.... You don't remember. Well, never mind about that, for now...."

"Yes, we've other things to attend to. You see, I *have* been celibate—and for too long...."

Within seconds, she'd torn my shirt off and pinned me to the bed. Then had my pants open. I was glad then that I'd followed Clio's advice and taken a shower. Sesbania had always found my perspiration arousing—but there were limits.

Her nimble fingers had soon brought me to the brink, then pulled me toward her.... Worried I was too far along, I spun her around and took my customary position.

"Oh, my," she giggled. "Now I know what she meant by exotic...."

Apparently, she really *had* lost her memory. For us, the scenario had been a familiar one. But then her subconscious must have taken hold, because just as usual in these circumstances, while one hand kneaded my head, the free one began slapping the wall. As you can imagine, it was a habit that often led to awkward encounters in hotels where walls are thin.

In this case, fortunately, it was an outside wall. But after a while, she switched hands. Now it was the locker beside the bed she slapped. With each stroke, a metallic *whomp* echoed about the room. Then came one particularly loud *whomp* and it seemed as if the entire ship shuddered.

"What was that?" she asked.

"Wasn't it you?"

"No, of course not."

Another *whomp* and the ship swung abruptly to starboard. I was tossed to the floor, and Sesbania against the metal locker. She was out cold. I placed her head on the pillow. She seemed to be breathing fine, but I couldn't wake her.

After dressing hurriedly, I joined Horatio in the control room. Mattie, his seamstress and inamorata, stood beside him. They were both staring open-mouthed out into the dusk.

"What is it?" I asked.

"*The Midnight Sun*!" she said portentously.

"What sun? Seems to have set."

"*The Midnight Sun* is an airship," Horatio explained. "Always thought it just legend, but look!"

A huge black airship now loomed before us. It fired a round of goo, hitting one of the port engines and rendering it inoperative.

"Looks like the same ship that attacked Jack," I said.

"Then better say your prayers for him. And us too!"

"Why? Whose ship is it?"

"All I know is the captain is said to be the cruelest pirate in the air!"

Albertson joined us to report the obvious fact that all the engines had been immobilized.

"I guess now ya wish ya kept that offal!" he chided.

"No use," Horatio told him.

"Even Jack's animal heads had no effect," I added.

By then Dottie had appeared. She alone seemed unalarmed. Perhaps too busy attending to the turkey leg held to her mouth.

"Look! They're leaving," Mattie said.

The huge ship rose above us.

"No, they're just getting ready to send over a boarding party," Horatio told her.

"Perhaps you ladies should go to your cabins," I suggested.

"No. Not me." Mattie grabbed Horatio's arm tight.

"I think you better," he told her.

Dottie, on the other hand, left without a word, still working on her drumstick. Once they'd gone, Albertson drew his cutlass and sliced the air.

"We'll fight 'em to the death!" he announced. "They won't never touch ar women!"

"Well, *you* can fight 'em to the death," Horatio told him. "Me, I follow the wind." He licked a finger and held it up. "Wind says, women gotta make do just like the rest of us."

CHAPTER 2.

THE MIDNIGHT SUN

The great black ship hovered fifty feet above and to our starboard. With impressive precision, they swung over on ropes, five at once crashing feet-first through the windows of the control room and landing fully prepared for battle. One thing was certain: these were pirates who knew their geometry.

The first wave was followed immediately by a second, and then a third. Totally outnumbered, Horatio and I dropped our weapons and raised our hands. As did Albertson, a moment after his ear was grazed by a dagger. By then there must have been fifteen or twenty of them. While several went off to the upper decks, others broke into the nearby cabins. Dottie and Mattie were brought out. Then one of the bandits who'd entered my cabin returned and whispered something to the apparent leader.

Certain features of these pirates struck me as incongruous—and yet, oddly familiar. First, all but one were noticeably shorter than your average brigand. Second, there was a smoothness to their movements which seemed at odds with their vocation. And last, they'd by then been aboard for at least a full minute and not one of them had spat.

There could be little doubt about it—these were the same Amazons who'd raided the S.S. *Paris*.

Their clothing ran colorful and ragged, but not without a certain stylishness. They wore various types of headgear—an assortment of bandanas, a few tricornes, and several large conical felt hats. Just as on the *Paris*, most managed to obscure their more womanly parts. This time, however, there were a couple who chose instead to display their wares. And in another departure: on the *Paris* they'd all worn masks; this time, they didn't bother to don them, instead making plentiful use of war paint.

What still wasn't clear was their objective. Was this another press-gang? Or did they have something more frightening in mind?

Once her underling had finished whispering her report, the leader—who stood appreciably taller than the others—nodded at the member of her crew then holding a dagger to my throat. Her manner brought to mind a disappointed Roman empress at the Colosseum, her nod taking the place of the traditional thumbs-down.

"Wait!" I shouted. "I'm sure we can work out some arrangement. If it's women you want, I've some spares upstairs. All comely, and all battle-tested. So depending on your needs..."

The empress sent me a look that froze my marrow. She took off her felt hat and tossed it to a minion. Then, with an alluring shake of her head, she let fall the thick mane of jet-black hair which had been hidden within. She had a classic elegance about her. One that even the blood-red streaks gracing her cheeks and crass overabundance of eyeshadow failed to conceal. Given a thorough cleansing, she could, I imagined, be stunningly attractive. But not with her lips twisted in the matchless display of loathing which they exhibited just then.

Mercifully, she turned from me and went into my cabin. My keeper followed, shoving me along before her.

"Close the door," the chief commanded.

Sesbania had been turned on her side. A pirate who stood beside the bed flipped back the sheet covering her.

All eyes seemed to gravitate to her shapely bum and the distinctive five-spotted mole which adorned it.

"I thought as much," the headwoman said. Then she turned toward me. "Simpleton!"

The sheet was thrown back over Sesbania and we all four left the room. In the meantime, Clio and Melpomene had been escorted down by pirates.

"Is this it?" the raven-haired chieftain asked.

"No, there're others. But they're giving us some trouble...."

"What sort of trouble?"

Her query was answered when half a dozen more of the raiders joined us, several badly wounded.

"It's no use," one bearing a tourniquet on her upper arm reported. "They're well armed, and barricaded in. Fighting like fiends."

"Where's Antiope?"

No one responded, the newcomers all looking one to another, each hoping someone else would answer.

"*Well?*"

"It looks like... she's defected."

"*What?* She now finds men to her taste?" Her lips were twisted again.

"Actually, they're women. Real hellions...."

"Mortal Sins," I corrected, netting myself a sea of quizzical looks.

"Anyway, it's not them so much as the bathhouse they're building."

"Bathhouse?"

"Yes, it's still under construction, but the blueprints

are really impressive. There's to be a hot pool, a warm pool, and a cool—"

"*Forget the damned bathhouse!* Did you try the perfume on them?"

"Well, Antiope has that...."

"Damn. And we're running low." She turned to our group. "Look, you women are welcome to join us. Why not free yourselves?"

Melpomene, who'd been whimpering throughout, let out a wail.

"Oh, Christ. *Not you.* But you others... Well, how about it?"

"Aw, nuts ta that," Dottie told her. Somehow in the interim she'd acquired another turkey leg.

"Suit yourselves—fools!" She was not an empress to stint on the scorn. "All right, let's get out of here."

Five at a time, they grabbed their ropes and swung back to their ship, which had by then descended and hovered somewhat below *Lucy.*

When they'd all gone, Dottie asked who they were.

"She-pirates," Albertson told her.

"The crew of *The Midnight Sun*!" Horatio said.

"Tryphaena, Father's nicknamed their captain," Clio told us.

"Who's Tryphaena?"

"If you'd read your *Satyricon,* you'd know. She roams the sea, in search of pleasure."

"An Amazon?"

"Not according to Petronius. Our Tryphaena seems to be a variation on the theme. Father lives in fear of her. Afraid she'll undermine his patriarchy."

"What do we do now?" Horatio asked. "All the engines are frozen in whatever they shot at us."

"Some sort of confection, I bet," Mattie volunteered.

"There's no use trying to deal with it until morning, whatever it is," I said. "Maybe then we can steam it off."

"What's going on?" Sesbania emerged, wrapped in a sheet. Or, I should say, *faux* Sesbania arrived, *nearly* wrapped in a sheet. I pulled up the trailing corner to cover her mole.

"You had a mild concussion," I told her. "It might be better if you lie back down for a while."

She scanned the scene of shattered glass and anxious faces. I took her arm and led her back inside the cabin, then closed the door and sat her down on the bed.

"Why were all the windows broken?"

"We had some visitors. Amazon pirates."

"*Really?* And I missed it?"

"You were knocked out during their initial assault."

"What did they want?"

"To look at your bum."

She stared at me for a moment, then came a revelation. "Oh! You mean... they were looking for recruits?"

"Something like that."

"Well, I hope they took all your damn wives!"

"No such luck. The Muses were too faithful, and the Sins too fierce."

"Oh well." She lay down on the bed—then quickly sat up. "Didn't they like my bum?" She twisted her body and tried to survey it. "Hand me that mirror." I did and she inspected her backside. "I guess it isn't anything special."

Learning my bedmate was not the soulmate I thought her to be was disconcerting. But it did at least relieve my guilt concerning the harem upstairs. I gave

27

her backside a playful slap. The mole may have been misplaced, but the general form of the bum itself seemed identical to real Sesbania's, and I'd never found it wanting. I told her so, then licked the wounds her vanity had suffered, along with whichever of her parts happened to be in easy reach.

Having tripped over so many doppelgangers since the crossover, I can't say I was terribly surprised. But what had inspired her to impersonate Sesbania? There seemed only one plausible motivation: me, of course. Still, there were several questions yet to be answered. For one, how had she come upon so many intimate details?

What puzzled me most of all was her apparent sincerity. Being an old hand at con work, I could generally spot a fellow artiste with near infallibility. (Though there's no denying I'd let Bonnet outwit me, that was more the exception than rule.) This faux Sesbania, however, seemed devoid of guile; in fact, it was one of the things I'd found most suspicious about her. Could it be she honestly believed she *was* Sesbania? In a world of steam-powered airships—where Nova Scotia looms in the South Pacific, and Prince Edward Island is mythical—anything could fall within the realm of the possible.

Since there seemed nothing to be gained by confronting her, or telling the others, I decided to keep what I'd learned to myself. We fell asleep still engaged and it wasn't until after midnight that I awoke to a soft knock on the door. I dressed and opened it to Clio.

"Sorry to bother you, but you might want to go upstairs. Your harem is restless...."

"Oh... Ah... It's been a long day.... I think I need some time to recover...."

"No, no. I mean they're fighting! With that newcomer."

"I thought she was a willing defector?"

"She has something they want. She's quite strong, but I think they'll get the best of her soon.... I moved my things to the library so I can get some sleep. Good luck."

Having no real beliefs or principles of my own, I'd always been quite a capable peacemaker. But brokering a truce between an Amazon pirate and a gaggle of Mortal Sins would, under the best of circumstances, tax my talents. In slightly less favorable conditions, it could easily cost me my life.

All in all, there's much to be said for bachelorhood.

II

In the harem—the former oar deck, festooned now with Oriental rugs, brass lamps, and miscellaneous adornments assembled from my wives' trousseaux—chaos reigned.

The space had been turned into a maze of compartments, each sectioned off by damask drapery. Some of the rooms were given over to communal uses—those where they ate, smoked, played games, or simply tormented one another.

But the majority of the expanse had been parceled into bedchambers and sitting rooms, sized according to each girl's demeanor. Wrath, needless to say, held the largest chunk of real estate, while Sloth, Clio, and Melpomene had been relegated to a tiny dormitory, one so deep in the recesses of the labyrinth, I'd never managed to locate it.

Making navigation all the harder, the air ran thick

with the smoke from their myriad thuribles and hookahs. And just in case that wasn't disorienting enough, the mingled aromas of those were supplemented—but certainly not complemented—by the various perfumes and fragrances they applied to their persons. Never having visited a Casbah bordello, I hesitate to speak ill of them. But I suspect my seraglio was an apposite proxy.

As soon as I entered, Antiope introduced herself by bouncing a large vase off my forehead. What's more, she did it with one hand—the other being occupied with menacing Wrath. The nimble Amazon had cut the angry Sin's robe to shreds with her cutlass. A compact warrior, and by far the better swordswoman, she had her adversary backed into a corner. At her feet lay Envy, Sloth, Avarice, and Pride. Dead or alive, I couldn't tell. At least until Sloth let loose a reassuring yawn.

I then heard telltale weeping to my aft. Picking myself up off the floor, I found Melpomene hiding in the folds of the drapery. I joined her, then held a hand to her mouth until she composed herself.

"What's going on?" I whispered.

"Everything was fine—at first. The six of them getting along like a house on fire. She's every bit as disagreeable as they are. But did you notice the glass vial she wears about her neck?"

"No, I was rather preoccupied with the vase directed at my forehead. What about it?"

"Well, Avarice saw it and yanked it off of her. Then, naturally, Envy wanted it. I'm not sure in what order she knocked them out, but Antiope eventually wound up getting it back. Then when Pride saw what had become of her sisters, she cried something about the family honor and lunged for the pirate girl's throat. Antiope made short work of her. But no sooner had she done so than Wrath appeared."

"I'd never noticed her evincing much sympathy for her sisters."

"No—but neither is she one to pass up a good fight. They've been at it now for close to an hour—all horribly brutal."

"Couldn't you have snuck out with Clio?"

"Well, yes. But..."

"Ah. More grist for the mill?"

"It *is* my life's work, after all."

"Indeed. Well, you wait here and I'll see if I can subdue her somehow."

"Good luck. I'm sure you'll do fine."

Her confidence steeled me—but only until I remembered she'd like nothing better than to witness the tragic death of her husband and lover. By then, unfortunately, I'd already left the safety of the curtain and picked up an alabaster elephant. I'd planned to subdue the pirate with a quick blow to the back of the head, but evidently she had eyes there as well. Without turning to face me, she swung her cutlass directly for my raised arms. I managed to jerk out of the way just in time. But in doing so, I dropped the stone elephant on my own head.

When I awoke—which couldn't have been too long after—I saw Wrath standing triumphantly over the fallen Amazon. Apparently my distraction had allowed her to prevail. Meanwhile, Melpomene lay buried in the curtain, weeping. I suspect the blow with which Antiope had hoped to amputate my forelimbs had instead detached the drapery the Muse had been hiding in.

With one foot on the neck of her foe, Wrath let out a sustained cackle. This brought to life at least one of her sisters. Pride crawled over to the vanquished pirate and pulled the glass vial from around her neck. Very gingerly, she opened it. Then held it to her nose.

"Careful! It may be poison," her sister warned her.

It was not poison, however, but perfume. The moment Pride uncorked it, I recognized the scent of a very particular, very powerful female aphrodisiac. *Deux nuits d'excès,* it was called. Or in English: two nights of excess.

Wrath had grabbed the vial as soon as she'd issued her warning and quickly recapped it. But not before spilling a few precious drops on her sister, and several more on herself. For what seemed like minutes, they both looked dumbly at one another. During this time, their breathing became heavy; I could see the rise and fall of their chests. Then, very slowly, they both turned toward me.

I'd only experienced one, rather oblique, episode involving this drug. Some of you may recall that Sesbania had a stash she kept similarly about her. She was saving it, she'd told me, and ordered me never to lay a finger on it. One morning I did, giving her no more than a whiff. That hadn't netted two nights of excess. But for several hours she very definitely put me through my paces.

Without taking her eyes off me, Pride slowly lifted herself from the floor. She removed the ornate pin which secured her robe and tossed it aside. As the layered veil slipped seductively around her ankles, she held out a finger and gestured toward herself. I was being summoned. My heart quickened—whether from fear or anticipation, or some combination, I can't say. My first impulse was to leave the field of battle posthaste. Countering that instinct, however, was the memory of this vainest of Sins' reaction when I'd earlier scorned her advances. That error in judgment had brought about my sojourn out on the plank.

A weighty decision, all right, but one considerably lightened by the vision before me. There's no denying that Pride was one very attractive woman: shapely long legs, perfectly proportioned breasts, and bobbed red hair that curled inwardly at the shoulder. Her eyes weren't large, but the straight-cut fringe of bangs across her forehead gave them a prominence they might otherwise have lacked. Her lips too were modest, but nonetheless finely sculpted. And the sprinkling of freckles which dotted her face and upper body gave an honest hint of her fiery temperament.

Like a spirit possessed, I answered her call. As she turned and led me deeper into the harem, she treated me to a show, courtesy of her oscillating bottom. So thoroughly beguiled was I that only after some moments did I remember Wrath. I looked about and saw her following behind me. Her head was bent down slightly, and she seemed to be biting her lower lip. But her eyes were fixed firmly upon me. It took a second to notice all that, however, because she too had abandoned her robe.

There was no doubting it now—they were identical twins. It had always been obvious they bore a strong resemblance to one another: both were shapely, carrot-topped, and freckled. But Pride dressed herself with great taste, wore heeled sandals that augmented her height, and was always impeccably groomed. Wrath, in contrast, roamed about with filthy bare feet, seemed to have only one robe, and took not the slightest bother with presentation. She had the same color hair, but wore it cut raggedly just below her shoulders. I doubt seriously it had ever been confronted by a comb.

As a rule, I've found shapely long legs and perfectly proportioned breasts go a long way toward mitigating petty matters of hygiene. Yet temptation and trepidation vied once more within me. One Deadly Sin is a handful; two Deadly Sins could prove—well, quite literally so.

Before long, I was utterly lost. Pride slipped through the drapes of one room after another, with me hot on her heels, and Wrath bringing up the rear—still biting her lip and still gazing upon me with a frightening intensity. By now, of course, I regretted not having ceded the field at the first sniff of that perfume. But it was too late. Retreat would mean a confrontation with Wrath, and though she'd doffed her robe, she still carried the cutlass with which she'd vanquished the Amazon. My only hope was that she'd somehow lose her way and I'd be left with just Pride to contend with.

Before I knew it, I was doing just that. No sooner had I followed her through a brocaded depiction of satyric revelry than she was upon me, and I found myself enjoying one of my own. The room wasn't a large one. But its entire expanse was taken up by a circular bed. I'd only just got under way when Wrath entered and my duties doubled. First one, then the other, now both at once....

Here, I'm afraid, I must pause. I've tried, as you well know, to keep this account as frank as possible. Partly because that's my nature, but also with an eye toward sales. Nonetheless, there are limits. Though I'm not easily embarrassed, providing a candid account of all that went on that night—or even a cherry-picked selection— just isn't feasible. Not that I've forgotten, mind you. Every moment of that scorching encounter—yea, every position, every combination, every ecstasy, every torture—is etched indelibly on my memory. (And more than a few on my very flesh.)

The problem is, rather, that providing a forthright catalogue of those entertainments would tax both *my* vocabulary and *your* credulity. Not that I'd blame you. Had I not been there myself, I too would doubt much of it even possible. I can, however, offer some broad observations to give you the general flavor.

First, Sins generally—and these twins particularly—are astonishingly supple. They can bend and stretch themselves in ways you'd think contrary to the laws of Nature. Second, the word inhibition is simply not in their dictionary. Third, and most surprising, there are occasions when they exhibit a real willingness to please. Rare occasions, of course, and unfortunately this characteristic is largely offset by my fourth observation: nothing titillates a Sin so much as inflicting a little pain. On the positive side, that titillation inevitably led to another cycle of uninhibited gymnastics and fresh ministrations.

III

With the rising of the sun, Pride and sister Wrath slipped into a mutual slumber. I won't tell you the precise position they were in, but suffice it to say, you'll not see this one among Maxfield Parrish's depictions of supine females. After some moments lost in study, I dressed and made a wary exit.

My principal fear was that one or more of the other girls had awoken and come upon the perfume left behind at the scene of carnage. To call my state at that time delicate would be an extreme understatement. After my beating at the hands of Pensacola rum-runners [Ed. note: see Book One], I pronounced them the champions of physical violence. Oh, what a naïf I was then!

I spent about an hour looking for a way out. Eventually, I happened upon Avarice, happily sound asleep, and five minutes later, Envy in a similar state. I didn't see Sloth, but I hardly needed to in order to assume she was likewise engaged. Then I came upon Melpomene, herself navigating the maze. She looked thoroughly exhausted.

"I've been tending Antiope. Wrath nearly killed her with that last blow." The tears came readily now. "We may need to get her to a hospital. Or at least find her a doctor.... We can't let her die!"

No doubt she was hoping to book the pirate girl for a return bout with her half-sisters.

"All right," I said. "But first I need to see about making the ship operable."

She dropped something from the folds of her robe. I reached down and picked it up. It was the vial of perfume.

"Maybe it would be better if I hung onto this, seeing all the trouble it's caused."

Her face flushed with uncharacteristic color; she was, in her own quiet way, incensed. That it had been the source of strife was precisely *why* she wanted it.

"Yes. All right," she said through gritted teeth.

Given my state, I hoped to convince faux Sesbania I'd spent the night subduing Antiope. She was absent from the cabin when I entered and I took the opportunity to lock up the love philtre in a drawer of the desk. She returned just in time to see me remove the key.

She cheerfully washed my wounds, and even refrained from asking awkward questions about the more implausible ones. Then she unnecessarily reminded me that Horatio would be expecting me to help with the freeing of the engines. If she had anything like the curiosity of her authentic counterpart, she'd have the drawer open ten seconds after I left the cabin. Then she'd dose herself and get into God knows what kind of mischief. The image of her in bed with Albertson flashed briefly before me.

On the way out, I unlocked the drawer and took the vial. She said nothing. But her mien transmuted into a thoroughly convincing impression of real Sesbania irked.

I found Horatio in the boiler room shouting encouragement to Albertson, who'd climbed out to one of the starboard engines. He'd been tethered by a length of rope and was chipping at the hardened goo with a pickaxe.

"He's liable to damage the engine with that, isn't he?" I asked.

"Maybe, but this won't be coming off any other way." He handed me a piece of the material that had been chipped off.

"Like obsidian."

"Not that bad. If you get it hot enough, it will melt."

"Then can't we use steam to loosen it?"

"Sure. But Percival took all the extra piping for his bathhouse."

"Well, we just need to take some back."

"Tried. But that pirate girl is up there with him. She didn't like my idea. Feel." He leaned his head forward. He had a bump on his skull about the size of the one the same young lady had given me on my forehead. "You gonna marry her too?"

"Don't be absurd. I'll go up and have a talk with Percival."

I hadn't spoken with the steamfitter since the night he came aboard, and even then we simply exchanged pleasantries. But he seemed a perfectly reasonable type.

Antiope, on the other hand, was anything but. And it was she who greeted me at the top of the ladder.

"*Whattaya want?*" she asked—in the most grating, high-pitched voice I've ever had the misfortune to experience. In case her attitude toward my intrusion was still in any doubt, she held her bloodied cutlass over her shoulder, poised to strike off my head if my answer fell short of expectations.

Her pirate costume was in shreds, bandages covered a full third of her body, and she stood at least a foot shorter than me. I'd taken the precaution of bringing my own cutlass, but hesitated to raise it. However diminutive, she was a Goliath of menace.

She wore her wiry mop in a style similar to Wrath's. It looked almost black, but it was difficult to discern its true color beneath the grease and grime she appeared to use as hair tonic. Her tattered bodice was merely perfunctory; one or both breasts were nearly always on display, the nipples erect and threatening. By no stretch could she be called pretty, or handsome, but she did exhibit a certain radiance whenever she smelled blood. Her eyes became wild and a strange half-smile formed upon her lips. Which is exactly the look she evinced at that moment. A distraction seemed in order.

"Sorry to bother you—I just thought I ought to introduce myself. E. Pluribus Van Slyke, captain of the airship *Lucy's Revenge*. Antiope, isn't it?"

I held out my hand and she spat on it.

"I thought you might be looking for that glass vial of yours."

"You got it?"

"No, but I believe I saw it in the harem. I passed through their little gambling den and spotted it sitting on the faro table. A forgotten wager, perhaps? It's not hard to find. From the entrance, three lefts, right, left again, two more rights, and then straight ahead through the hair salon."

She lowered her blade. "How do I know this ain't a trick?"

"Trick? To what end?"

"How should I know! But don't matter. If yer lyin', I'll be back for ya!"

She pushed her way past me. What sort of mayhem I might have set in motion was impossible to know, but it seemed plausible to suppose she'd be occupied for a good little while.

With it now appearing safe to proceed, I went looking for Percival. And very soon found him. Or, rather, he found me. Like a back-alley brigand, he dropped on me from above wielding a monkey wrench.

You wouldn't think a plumber armed with a monkey wrench much of a match for a naval officer bearing a sword, but he was a much abler plumber than I was a naval officer. One of the many mementos I have from that voyage is the crook he gave my heretofore unblemished nose.

He had me down, but just as he came in for the kill, he was distracted by a noise behind him. I picked up a short length of pipe and dispatched him.

Melpomene emerged from the shadows and knelt down beside him, weeping.

"What's gotten into him?" I asked.

"Somehow he found out you had your way with me in the loft."

"What business is that of his?"

"Oh, he's always been in love with me.... But it just wasn't meant to be."

"Has he turned violent before?"

"Only the once.... Poor Lionel." Now the floodgates opened.

"Who's Lionel?"

"*Was,* I'm afraid. The first husband Father picked out for me. Seemed a perfect match. A choirmaster who suffered from chronic depression."

"Sounds ideal. But Percival objected?"

"Yes—with a hacksaw.... It really was awful—so gruesome.... We never found one of the arms...."

"How horrifying. And yet you thought it all right to bring him along here?"

"*Well,* I couldn't be *sure* the same thing would happen...."

No, she couldn't have been sure. But it might have seemed a reasonably sound bet. "I don't suppose you happened to have mentioned to him what went on in the loft?"

"Whyever would you think that?"

Whyever, indeed. You look upon someone who spends her days weeping and you naturally assume she's some variety of cream puff. But look a little deeper and you'll see a cunning Muse who feeds on misery. If supplies run short, she's always willing and able to cook up some herself.

After tying up Percival, I summoned Horatio and Albertson and we re-requisitioned the piping necessary to steam-clean the engines. We were just carrying off the last of it, when Antiope reappeared.

I thought she'd done a superlative job with the menacing look before. But on seeing Percival knocked out and bound, she took it to new heights. She snarled and yowled, like a cat in heat, waved her cutlass in a circle above her head, and then charged me like a mad rhino.

"You bastard!" she screeched—though in her rendering there were several extra, excruciating syllables.

Fortunately, the Fates were with me that morning (I speak only figuratively, of course). Through sheer luck, and luck alone, Albertson laid her low. He'd been toting a long length of pipe on his shoulder and pivoted to see what the commotion was about. The crazed Amazon rushed headlong into the cast-iron conduit.

We tied her up as well, then positioned her beside Percival. Before leaving, I dabbed a few drops of the perfume on her. With luck, she'd give Percival such a workout he'd forget all about my miserable Muse.

Then I had second thoughts. According to the lore real Sesbania had passed on to me, once a woman had had her two nights of excess, the elixir became nothing more to her than a pleasant scent. Since she carried it on her person, it seemed unlikely Antiope hadn't had her allotment. But if it now had no effect on her, why did she treasure it so? Then the obvious answer came to me: for an Amazon, an aphrodisiac which worked on *other* females would have its uses.

Still, nothing ventured, nothing gained.

It took all that day and half the night to free up the engines. But eventually we got them all running, and with the sun at its height, made excellent time.

We had no more trouble from Antiope. What precisely occurred once she and Percival both awakened is impossible to say. But not long afterward, eerie, cat-like howls began emanating from the former gun deck.

CHAPTER 3.

THE MANICURIST IS IN

By the time we had her under way again, *Lucy* had drifted eastward several hundred miles. We were now somewhere over the North Carolina piedmont and at least twelve hours from the Lafittes' haven in Barataria.

"You incompetent ass!"

If you're partial to spouses who whisper sweet nothings, my advice is to avoid Sins categorically. Billing and cooing simply aren't part of the repertoire. A Sin's talents lie elsewhere. They're very good at abuse generally, and veritable virtuosi of faultfinding and belittling. On good days, this might be limited to a contumelious remark, or the odd expostulation of disgust; on bad days, it's one long invective, an endless stream of captious vituperation from morning to night. What's worse, Sins are rarely at a loss for words.

"You imitation of a ship's captain! Mockery of a man! Sagging blossom of a husband!"

This was Avarice expressing her dismay at our having been delayed. She sat sprawled on her couch, her robe loose about her. The hour was late, long after midnight, but she showed no sign of fatigue.

"It's hardly my fault we were attacked by those Amazons," I said by way of defense.

"You should have evaded them! A proper captain would have! But you were too busy accepting the favors of one of your wives, weren't you?"

"Well..."

"And I doubt you even managed to bring *that* off!"

"That's not fair.... We were interrupted."

"Shut up! Thanks to you we lost two days. Father might even get to Barataria before us...."

"Then perhaps it would be wise to alter our plans. We could head directly to Tortuga. It wouldn't take much longer."

"No! You sniveling coward! We need to stick to the plan. We'll just have to hope he's delayed himself.... Yes— of course! He'll stop in New York to sell that liquor you let him cheat you out of—any idiot should have seen that coming. When will we reach Louisiana?"

"Not until tomorrow afternoon. Three at the earliest, more likely four or five."

"All right. That will have to do. In the meantime, I suggest you work on developing some backbone."

"What I really need is some sleep."

"Sleep?" she said with the customary look of contempt, but in a tone which betrayed a modicum of disappointment. "Well, then I've no use for you." She pulled her robe over an exposed thigh. "Go."

I assumed she'd summoned me to her apartment merely for her own convenience. But it now appeared she'd anticipated making further use of my ready tongue. It simply hadn't occurred to her that a torrent of ridicule might not be the best way to set the mood for an amorous dalliance. Frankly, I didn't mind in the least forgoing another bout with her. It came too close to hard labor.

I was exhausted. But what I needed even more than sleep was a thorough scrubbing. Steam-cleaning an airship is hot, sticky work. There were three places to bathe on board. A sizable bathroom Percival had jury-rigged in the harem (not to be confused with the palatial bathhouse still under construction on the deck above), the original crew's shower room, and a large washtub used by Sesbania and Mattie because they weren't permitted to use option one and were too repulsed by option two. So it was only Horatio and myself who made use of the shower room. What accommodation Dottie or Albertson made for bathing was something of a mystery, and one probably best left unexplored.

I took a long, hot shower, then made my way to my cabin. Mere seconds after I entered, faux Sesbania did as well. There was a look in her eye I recognized. A singularly determined look. I felt the pockets of my trousers and found that the vial had disappeared; the little imp had searched my clothes while I showered.

Well, I had a pretty good idea what she had in mind, and knew there'd be little to no chance of dissuading her. So, what the hell—I entered into the spirit of the thing.

I don't know what kind of shape she'd been in before her abduction, but from all appearances, she was fully recovered from the ordeal. What's more, I now felt certain that this was *not* the girl I'd lost from the S.S. *Paris*. Real Sesbania had her moments of unbridled passion, but not once had she dislocated my arm. Faux Sesbania did not only that; with a second, equally alacritous move, she popped it back into place. And all the while providing artful distraction from the pain.

It was a stellar performance, all right. But the very moment the sun streamed through the porthole, she collapsed into a deep sleep. It hadn't been the advertised full night of excess. However, speaking for myself, it was plenty. One thing was sure: for the safety of the ship, it was imperative that I maintain control of the provoking perfume.

I made a quick search of the outfit she'd doffed so

adroitly on entering the cabin. At first, I found nothing. But there, in the pleats of her skirt, was a hidden pocket. Faux Sesbania or not, she was a sly little minx. Before rejoining her on the pillow, I took the precaution of concealing the vial in the sole of my shoe. I've never bought a pair of shoes without hollowing out a small hiding place in each of the heels. A few gold coins, or a pair of loaded dice, often come in handy. So often, the hollows were almost always empty and available. Real Sesbania, of course, knew about this habit of mine. But she was still whereabouts unknown.

The plan put forward by Avarice for the raid on Barataria followed that which we'd used so successfully in St. Pierre. Once a month or so, mad Captain Bonnet made the rounds of his string of barrooms named for abused pelicans. On arrival, he'd send his son-in-law and Avarice to collect the profits. This son-in-law, a fellow named Smedley, happened to be a near twin of myself. So it was just a matter of us getting there first and collecting the loot. We'd done well in St. Pierre, and she claimed Barataria would be better still.

That suited me. I'd lost out on an enormous amount of money since that fateful evening aboard the S.S. *Paris.* There was the fifteen thousand sewn into the lining of Sesbania's chemise, the twenty-five thousand Rutledge had offered for the return of his daughter, the ten thousand in jewels used to buy my freedom in Nassau, and lastly, the like amount in gold used to purchase *Lucy*— the dearest hooker on either side of the fictional divide.

Avarice called for me about four that afternoon. She took one look at faux Sesbania, still asleep on the bed, and curled a lip. Anatomically, Sins are indistinguishable from other women—with one small area of exception.

They seem to have an extra set of muscles arrayed about the lower face which allows them to twist and turn their lips into every possible nuance of derision.

"You still look a mess," the greedy Sin told me. "That redheaded duo really worked you over, didn't they? We'll need some story to explain all those bruises. Ah—we can tell them you've just visited Clarisse in Tortuga."

"In that case maybe I should garnish myself with a little *crème fraîche* and gravy."

She didn't get my joke, but I imagine she'd never shared a meal with Clarisse. Or, come to think of it, shared much of anything with anybody. Which is why I brought up our split.

"Last time, I agreed to take a meager quarter share. But included with that was your help in freeing Sesbania. I think I deserve an equal half this time."

"Well, if you insist. But should you, I think I might let slip to Pride your assessment of her lovemaking."

"I've never said a word."

"Really? I remember you telling me she was like a wet fish. And what was it you called her eyes? Beady, wasn't it? Oh, I don't think she'll care for that...."

We settled on a seventy-thirty split. A small victory, perhaps, but my adversary was ruthless to the extreme.

I'd hoped to bring Albertson along to reprise his role as Geoff l'Indigné, Lafitte's henchman. But since his domestication at the hands of Dottie, he'd become a shadow of his former brutal self. It'd been almost a week since he'd even punched a man.

In his stead, Avarice suggested we bring along Pride, Wrath, and Envy to create a diversion.

"You mean, send them directly into the pirates' nest? That might be a bit dangerous—vicious though they are."

"Nothing so foolhardy. We'll send them shopping. Every pirate port has a selection of jewelry stores."

"I've noticed that buccaneers have a penchant for trinkets."

"Yes, and the Lafittes' band particularly so."

"But will shopping be much of a diversion?"

"Shopping's always been a source of fun for them. You saw them at the auction house. I remember once, when we were just children, Father took us into Manhattan. Took years for Fifth Avenue to recover."

As fantastic as it sounded, I took her at her word. God help the store clerk who stood between a willful Sin and the bauble she admired.

We moored at the far end of town alongside a number of other airships. As darkness fell, the wives and I made our way along the well-trodden path. Two pirates coming from the opposite direction, both drunk, made insulting inquiries of the girls. I went up to the smaller of the two and conked him on the back of the head with the butt of my cutlass. Before he even hit the ground, Wrath had subdued his companion. Then, within seconds, my Sins quite purposefully stripped them of valuables—and, quite gratuitously, of several organs. If we were ever to socialize as a family, Wrath would need to be broken of her habit. It's hard to imagine any formal gathering where the filleting of guests wouldn't be taken amiss.

While her sisters disappeared into a jeweler's, Avarice and I continued on to *Le Pélican Stupéfait* just two doors down. She'd told me the manager was a large, friendly fellow, which came as a relief. I'd visited The Stupefied Pelican during my previous sojourn in Barataria and had most definitely not met anyone even remotely friendly. So there seemed no reason this fellow wouldn't accept me as Smedley.

He took us into a back room and fed us sautéed prawns while he retrieved his weighty money box. Business had been brisk, and even a third of the profits—our just share—amounted to well over ten thousand in gold. A satisfying sum, I thought. And he really was a likable fellow. More to the point, I wasn't looking forward to having to battle our way out of town should things not go as planned. The odds of the Lafittes letting me slip through their hands a second time I estimated at infinitesimal.

With that as my train of thought, I suggested to Avarice—sotto voce—that we take only the cut her father was due. Her mouth narrowed, her brow furrowed, and the fingernails of her left hand took several layers of flesh from the back of my right one. We were halfway to being one of those couples who need no words to communicate... *her* half.

"The girls will have started their riot by now," she whispered. "The barroom will be all but empty. Go out and create a disturbance, just enough to draw him out of the room."

"A disturbance?"

As she reached for my other hand, I rose from the table and excused myself.

The barroom was, indeed, nearly empty—only the bartender and three patrons remaining. Unfortunately, one of the three bore a striking resemblance to Albertson. Which meant he was none other than Jean Lafitte's henchman, Geoff l'Indigné. Not only had we met during my previous stopover, but Jack Tigue and I had given him plenty new to be indignant about.

He cackled on seeing me, then issued instructions to his companions in French. Rather ominously, these instructions once more included the term *le cachot,* which I had learned the old-fashioned way translated to something in the neighborhood of torture chamber.

II

I saw a window and ran for it. There's a technique to exiting a barroom quickly and it usually involves diving headfirst through a window. Risky business if it happens to be closed, as some are more carefully constructed than others. But since building codes are a rarity in pirate ports, I assumed this one would give way easily. And, thankfully, it did.

I landed in the usual mire of mud and filth. Which is one of the reasons this manner of exit works so well. There's nearly always a cesspool in the alley outside barrooms of a certain grade. For many fellows—pirates, not surprisingly, chief among them—urinating alfresco is an integral part of fraternal fun.

As it happened, I recognized this particular cesspool from my last visit. And likewise the masonry stairs just beyond which led down to the Lafittes' dungeon. Thus motivated, I picked myself up and ran for the far end of the alley. It dead-ended onto another alley, and from there I could go in only one direction. And only another thirty yards. Ahead was a blank wall twenty feet high, and to my right, the Lafittes' mansion. I tried the building on the left side, but it was locked up tight, with the windows twelve feet up from the ground. I managed to shatter one with a brick, but I couldn't find any suitable handholds to climb up to it.

Now Geoff l'Indigné could be heard cackling from just around the corner. With no other options available, I went quickly to the Lafittes' house opposite. There was an open window facing the porch and I crawled through it before my pursuers were on the scene. They'd heard me shatter the window and now assumed I'd somehow found a way up to it. While one man stayed behind to keep watch, the others went off in search of an easier means of entering that building.

I was safe for the moment, but that wasn't likely to last long. I went about looking for another avenue of egress, one without a pirate standing guard. The house was a warren of oddly divided rooms, all in disrepair, and most with windows either boarded up or barred with ironwork. The only free windows I found looked out on a porch on the opposite side of the house. There a gaggle of the Lafitte crew sat drinking and cackling their approval of the riot spilling out of the nearby jeweler's.

For the present, I was trapped. I'd simply have to wait until I could make my exit undetected. In the meantime, I needed a safe place to hide. I came upon a pantry off of the kitchen, and a well-stocked storeroom off of that. There I constructed a comfortable little hiding place by rearranging the assorted beer kegs, casks of brandy, and sacks of flour. At last, I could catch my breath—even take a short nap.

I woke to the sounds of men in the kitchen. Then heard one coming into the storeroom itself. My pulse quickened. And when he picked up one of the casks of brandy, I thought my heart would explode. I prepared to spring on him. But miraculously, he missed seeing me. Presumably, his eyes hadn't adjusted to the semidarkness. A close call if ever there was one.

Once he'd gone, I managed to get control of my fears and relax. My respite, however, proved to be a brief one. Someone shouted instructions in French and I distinctly heard the word *bière*. Then footsteps. The beer kegs formed the very foundation of my fortress—take one of those and it was good-bye Pluribus. I looked about for a means of escape. A wooden ladder in the far corner of the room led up to a trapdoor. I was up it and through the hatch in a matter of seconds.

It entered onto a tiny chamber, just large enough for me to fold myself up in—but not enough room to close the trapdoor. And this time, the pirate turned on a light. While he uncovered the beer, I held my breath, frozen.

Mercifully, he didn't look up. Once he'd selected a keg, he rolled it out and doused the light. Now in total darkness, I felt about the chamber and found a latch. Then, on the opposite side, hinges. The roof of the chamber could be opened. As quietly as possible, I unlatched and lifted it. The room it opened onto was almost as dark as the chamber. But there was little time to assay it before someone hit me on the head.

"Ow," I said.

"I'll kill myself before giving myself up to you!"

Then she hit me again, harder. I reached over and took the shoe from her.

"Look," I told her, "if it's any comfort, I'm not with the pirates. I'm trying to evade them myself."

"Then why did you hide in the chest?"

"What chest?"

I could see then that the chamber I'd emerged from appeared on the outside to be a large seaman's chest.

"It seems this chest also hides passage to the floor

below," I explained. "I take it you're one of the Lafittes' captives?"

"Yes. The devilish fiends! ...But I suppose that's what I get for hitchhiking."

"Hitchhiking?"

"I was trying to get to Nassau. You see, I'm looking for a friend."

"And this friend is living in Nassau? I stopped by there a couple weeks back and I can't say I recommend the place. Especially if you harbor a dislike for devilish fiends."

"Full of brigands?"

"How full of them, I can't say. But they do seem to run the place."

"Well... this friend I'm looking for may have gone a little... piratey."

"Piratey?"

"I couldn't think of the proper adjective."

"Perhaps it's a mere coincidence, but I met a pirate a week or so ago who was looking for a lost friend. Your pirate wouldn't happen to be Jack Tigue, would it?"

"You know Jack?"

"Well, we broke bread together. Very hospitable guy. Lays a wonderful table." Not knowing just what sort of friends they were, I left Celia and the rest of Jack's concubines unmentioned.

"Yes, he's always been like that—provided he likes you, of course. Otherwise..."

"Say no more. I've seen the otherwise. Are you hoping to get him to give up his pirate ways?"

"Jack? Oh, I don't know about that. We tried for years to get him to tame his temper. But then someone would say, or do, something, and, well... quick as a blink...."

"Yes, he doesn't waste much time on deliberations. If it's any consolation, he's not a terribly unreasonable pirate. Just takes the chivalry thing very seriously."

"He always has.... That's why he ended up going off to the circus...."

"Ah. I read about that."

"Did you really?"

"Yes, in a strange little book, *The Circensiad*."

"How in the world did you come across that?"

"My cousin claims it was sent to her so she could give it a rewrite."

"Oh. How very odd. Well, *I* wrote it!"

"So you're Eugenia?"

"Yes, Eugenia Biddle. And you?"

"E. Pluribus Van Slyke."

"What a ridiculous—"

"Yes, I know. But it can't be helped." I could tolerate a fair amount of ribbing about my queer name, but it seemed out of line coming from a fictional character. Especially one with a name like hers. "Anyway, we should set aside the literary memoir for now and concentrate on how we might get away from here. Tell me, if you didn't know there was a passage leading to the chest, why were you there waiting to subdue me?"

"Well, a pure and innocent woman... locked in her chamber with a chest not belonging to her.... Naturally, I just assumed some dastardly knave was waiting to emerge and have his way with me—or at least purport to have had his way with me. Which amounts to nearly the same thing...."

"Oh. Because of the literary precedent?"

"Yes, exactly. Boccaccio's *Decameron* is one of my favorites; *Cymbeline*, however, I can take or leave."

"Interesting. Well, if I might offer a little advice, the next time you find yourself keeping sentinel at a chest, avail yourself of something a little more lethal than a soft shoe."

"Yes, I see what you mean. Heels would be better. But these are so much more comfortable traveling.... Piratical, I'll bet."

"Piratical?"

"The adjectival form of pirate."

Typical of her species, this literary damsel seemed stunningly ill-prepared for the adventure she'd set out upon. With her little half-moon eyeglasses and blonde hair pulled back in a loose ponytail, she looked like a schoolmarm—albeit a young and attractive schoolmarm.

"I suggest we wait until they finish their meal and then make our exit the way I came in. What time is supper served?"

"Last night, not until eleven. They're very late risers, so everything is later accordingly."

"That's three hours from now. Until then, we'll just need to occupy ourselves as best we can...." I said this with all the suggestion it could bear and still fall short of vulgar. But she wasn't biting.

"I've some playing cards...."

So we played gin rummy while she told me about her childhood and family. Though I didn't tell her so, I was already familiar with much of it, from Cousin Emmie's books. Eugenia's telling made it sound not quite so fantastic, nor was her word choice so florid. And there wasn't a single mention of Walt Whitman's pond snipe.

Just after eleven, there was a soft knock on the door. Eugenia opened it and brought in a large tray covered in enticing dishes and a half-bottle of white wine. As soon as the door closed, I could hear it being locked and barred on the outside.

We agreed we should eat what we could while we had the chance, and she was quite generous about sharing her food. The pâté was excellent, though to be honest, the duck in the terrine tasted a little dry. And I had a hard time getting any of the wine. She told me she had best brace herself and the wine would help.

A half-hour later, I opened the chest and went down to reconnoiter. It was dark, and the house seemed to be empty. I went back for Eugenia and found her a little overly braced. She had difficulty descending the ladder, then tripped over a mop bucket.

There was some shouting in the distance. But eventually things quieted and we proceeded into the kitchen. The dinner dishes had been piled up to be washed later and it was one of these stacks that Eugenia now backed into. More shouting. And then, footfalls....

I opened the door of a walk-in cooler and pushed her inside. "Wait here a minute and I'll divert them."

I returned to the back of the house and the window I'd entered through earlier that evening. I smashed it with my elbow, then retreated to an adjoining room. More shouts and footfalls. Once again, my diversion seemed to have worked. The pirates looked at the window and deduced we'd exited via it. Three of them ran out into the alley in search of us.

But not the fourth. He, sadly, was not so gullible. He tried the window and saw it wasn't locked. Then he rubbed his chin with his hand, as pirates are wont to do. I was no more than seven or eight feet from him, hiding around the doorway. There was a second door leading from the room I was in and I tiptoed for that.

I don't know if you've ever tried tiptoeing in a house which has been occupied by inattentive pirates since the antebellum era, but your odds of doing it noiselessly are nil. The pirate who'd been rubbing his chin swiftly spun around and sent a dagger into the door I'd set course for. Figuring I now had nothing to lose, I ran for it.

It was locked. And my old friend Geoff l'Indigné was instantly upon me.

III

He cackled first, of course. But I suppose he had every right to. Next, he said something I couldn't quite make out, cackled again, and seemed to be waiting for a reply. In my very best college French, I told him he looked well.

Whether he detected some insincerity in my tone, or perhaps noticed my glance at the stump which had been his right pinkie, I can't say with certainty. But one way or another, I'd annoyed him. Which he conveyed by slamming his forehead into mine.

I awoke strapped to the same means of torture Geoff had introduced me to during my previous stay with him. He stood by with a couple of his subordinates and they promptly broke into a round. Geoff started things off, then the pirate on his left joined in, and finally the pirate on his right. There were few actual words to the song, the lyrics consisting mainly of cackles.

Once they'd finished the fifth verse, Geoff switched on the diabolical machine—an ingenious contraption which I described in detail earlier [Ed. note: see Book One]. My hand was strapped to a pivoting metal plate, with a blade coming down just an inch or so from the tips of my fingers. After each ping of the blade, the plate would pivot with a click, and then a whoosh and the blade would move a little closer to my fingers. But the real genius of the thing lay in the manner in which it was propelled. With my slightest movement, another cycle would begin. Struggling against the straps would send it into a frenzy, and even breathing carried a risk.

It had been a sneezing fit which had nearly done me in during the last session, and on that count, things didn't appear auspicious. The room seemed just as filthy as before, and another fit all but inevitable. The one thing working in my favor was that this day was a good deal damper. With a little luck, that would keep the dust settled.

But these brigands, as clever as they were cruel, had not been resting on their laurels. They'd managed to improve their design. Geoff shouted some query. He asked me, I believe, if I found things a little warm. Before I could answer, he turned on an electric fan!

Then he flicked off the lights and the three of them exited the room, coughing. Cackling, too, of course, but the coughing predominated. And for me as well, which naturally sent the machine into high gear—*cough, ping, click, whoosh, cough, ping, click, whoosh, cough, ping, click, whoosh....*

It went on for what seemed like hours. Aside from the coughing, I felt paralyzed with fear and so distracted by terror a full minute passed before I realized someone had switched off the fan. Had Jack, while making his regular rounds rescuing maidens in distress, taken the time to save me once more? Quickly, I tried to formulate some excuse for having abandoned him in his hour of peril.

"It was my crew! They mutinied! I couldn't do a thing about it, Jack!"

"*Jees-us!* What the hell are ya jabberin' about? And what are you doin' here?"

It wasn't Jack, but that most unlikely of rescuers, a newspaper journalist, one Augusta Ready. And she was looking nothing if not piratical: the regulation silk apparel bearing a collection of tears, cuts, and stains; and the hitherto immaculate body exhibiting more than a few as well.

With the air settling once more, my coughing had subsided. As had my agitation at the thought of having to confront Jack. But the monstrous manicuring machine had only slowed.

"I'd be happy to give you a complete rundown of events since our last meeting, but perhaps in the meantime you could switch this thing off."

"I don't know.... Seein' you in pain might be kinda fun...."

"Not universally...."

"Say, you got a way outta here? I mean, out of Barataria?"

"If I hurry. *Lucy's Revenge* is moored just outside of town."

"Then maybe we can make a deal." She switched off the instrument of torment and started unstrapping me. "I'm aimin' to lam it out of here myself."

"You're always welcome, but we'd better run."

"What's the matter? Afraid the crew will mutiny again?"

"Well, even if they were feeling uncharacteristically loyal, they now total just two, Horatio and Albertson. And they're outnumbered by... well, certain associates...

of a less-than-reliable nature.... Though to be fair, one can't accuse them of being inconstant.... Nonetheless, they're not governed by... by anything, really...."

"Whattaya, been goin' to law school? You can tell me on the way. Come on."

At the top of the stairs, she opened the door and looked about.

"The coast is clear. They should all be over at the Pelican by now."

"You sure *all* of them?"

"Yeah, there's a floor show Wednesdays. They never miss it."

"A cackling chanteuse?"

"How'd you know that?"

"Lucky guess."

She picked up a duffle she had waiting there and handed it to me. We were nearly to the door when I stopped her.

"I just remembered. I left a girl in the cooler."

"*You just remembered you left a girl in the cooler?* What the hell are you talkin' about?"

"In the kitchen. We were making an escape and I left her in the cooler to hide."

"An' yer just rememberin' now? Christ, yer somethin'. Is it that frumpy hitchhiker?"

"I wouldn't call her frumpy...."

"Well, you got strange taste."

She led the way back to the kitchen where the dishes sat undisturbed—save the stack Eugenia had upended earlier. I opened the door of the cooler.

"It's safe now to come out."

But Eugenia wasn't in the cooler. Nor the storeroom, nor the room she'd been held captive in.

"Guess she got away without you."

Given she'd had trouble navigating more than a few feet on her own, I thought that rather unlikely. I called her name.

"Whattaya, nuts?" Aggie asked while muffling me. "Come on, we gotta get out of here."

I had an unusually difficult time rationalizing my abandonment of the girl. Partly because I'd found her so likable, in a brother-sister kind of way. But mainly because, were Jack to find out I'd misplaced his friend, he might become irritated. And Jack knew only one way of resolving his irritation....

We were on our way back through the kitchen when two cooks came upon us. Aggie appeared to be on friendly terms with them and spoke to them at some length in French. From what I could gather, they were angry at being sent to do the dishes.

"These guys are looking to leave town," she told me. "You got room for a couple passengers?"

"If they can cook, sure."

"*If* they can cook? Emile's the saucier, an' Reynard's an ace pâtissier."

"Pâtissier?"

"Makes pastries, you gink."

They quickly gathered up a couple dozen knives, whisks, and copper pans and tossed these in a laundry bag. They insisted they needed nothing else, so we hurried out of the house.

"I know a shortcut," Aggie said.

It may have been shorter as the crow flies, but at the cost of a good deal of pain later. The too-narrow path ran through a thorny thicket, which included wild rose and a vine I couldn't identify in the dark, but later determined to be poison ivy. As I say, the pain arising from that would be felt only later. That arising from the sharp blow to my head was far more immediate.

A pair of free-lancing pirates had waylaid us. And the two cooks were nowhere to be seen. Having temporarily disabled me, the brigands now attempted to make off with my companion. A bad choice on their part. Had their inclinations run in the opposite direction, they might have had more success. Aggie gave one a deep gash across the face with her razor, then deftly removed the right thumb of the other. They were last seen heading for Barataria, where I expect there's a charity hospital geared toward sewing up the wounds of pirates.

I complimented her work with the blade. Even if it did lack the thoroughness of Wrath's, it was nonetheless impressive.

"Yeah, thanks. Now help me find it." She was on her knees in the brush.

"I can get you another razor."

"Not my razor! *His thumb!*"

It took us until nearly dawn to reach where *Lucy* was docked. Just as we arrived, Albertson descended and began unhitching the ship's mooring ropes.

"Not going to leave without me, were you?"

"We took a vote. That's just how it came out."

"Well, I'm vetoing the proposal. And I brought along an old comrade."

Aggie stepped from the shadows and Albertson gave her a wary look—most particularly, her necklace. Though its place had been taken by the bloody thumb of the pirate, he apparently hadn't forgotten the occasion when she'd done likewise with his finger.

We finished untying the moorings, then as the three

of us were being winched up, the two cooks appeared, making vague excuses about having gotten lost. I would have sent them on their way, but our fare until then had been no more than adequate, and never what might be called inspired.

And in case you're wondering, the vote had been eleven to one. Only faux Sesbania had elected to wait. But I took some additional comfort in the fact that both Mattie and Clio had abstained.

Chapter 4.

A Book's Worth of Revelations

At the insistence of Avarice, I set us on course for Tortuga and the next unhappy pelican. Given how close a call I'd had in Barataria, I considered the plan ill-omened. But she refused to give me my portion of the take until we arrived.

Once we were under way, I went in and hit the sack. Then about noon, faux Sesbania woke me with coffee and a plate of ham, eggs, and toast. It really didn't measure up to the chow the Lafittes served their houseguests, but the service was attentive and there's something to say for that.

An hour later, I emerged to find Horatio giving Aggie an account of our adventures since she left our company—Sins and Muses included.

"...That night, we all went down to St. Pierre, where the captain's wife..."

"His wife..." She looked over at me, her head atilt.

"First wife—"

"Skip it. I know about the rest."

She'd cleaned herself up during the interim and now sported an immaculate burgundy silk blouse over charcoal knee breeches, with an ivory sash about the waist and a tooled-leather headband. She still looked the pirate, but one with a strong sense of fashion. Even her disheveled mop now worked to her advantage. This was 1924, after all, and tomboy-chic the rage. The new scar above her right eye, however, may have taken things a bit far.

"That button on your sleeve looks about to fall off," I told Horatio. "Maybe you better have it attended to. I can take over."

"Aye, aye, sir."

He made one of his comic salutes and called for Mattie. She replied from the galley, informing him she was out of thread. He shrugged and went into their cabin alone.

"How you gettin' along with girlie in there?" Aggie asked. "She adjustin' to circumstances all right?"

"Oh, Sesbania's always been open-minded."

"Yeah? Ain't that swell.... So when do I get to meet this nutty harem of yours?"

"Well, they're at their least dangerous just after a big meal. I suggest waiting until later this evening."

"Suits me. Horatio told me about Jack Tigue. And how they cruised together in the old days. What'd you think of him?"

"Certainly unique. And a little more refined since his time with the circus. By the way, you met the authoress of that book."

"I thought your cousin wrote it?"

"She claims only partial authorship. The originator was that girl held at the Lafittes'."

"The one you left in the cooler?"

"Yes, that's the one. She also happens to be a friend of Jack's."

"You're kiddin'?"

"Childhood friends."

"Small world. Guess he won't be pleased you lost her."

"No. And I think I may have annoyed him some already."

"Horatio told me how you ran off when his back was against the wall."

"I wouldn't say ran off—just didn't find it convenient to stop...."

"You ain't much of a fighter, are you?"

"Well, when the time's ripe...." A change of subject seemed in order. "We heard a rumor you were traveling with brother Jean—and that he'd taken a liking to you."

"The cretin couldn't keep his hands off me...."

Just then, Sesbania (faux) emerged from our cabin. "Sorry, I didn't mean to interrupt." She went off toward the galley, hardly lifting her eyes from the floor.

"Ain't got much to say, does she?" Aggie asked.

"Just a little shy around strangers," I told her.

"I guess you got that in common."

"Getting back to your adventure... Lafitte took you with him on leaving Tortuga?"

"Yeah, he thought it pretty amusin', my abbreviatin' Geoff l'Indigné's little finger."

"Having spent time in his dungeon, I'd say he was partial to the abbreviating of digits generally."

"Yeah. Well, just the same, he said he'd have to flog me.... An' right there in the street.... Then when he saw I was female..."

"It must have been horribly humiliating, to be exposed like that."

"Well, at the time, the fear of havin' my flesh ripped open by the lash did a good job of keepin' the lid on the humiliation. But seein' how things were, he changed his mind and had me brought to his ship. Told me I'd be ransomed off. 'Course I knew that'd only be after having his way with me."

" So he forced himself on you?"

"Sure. He's a pirate, ain't he? That first night, he has me brought to his cabin...."

"You don't need to go into detail if it's painful."

"He had me half undressed.... But then I pulled the old Scheherazade...."

"Old Scheherazade?"

"The maiden who diverts the bloodthirsty sultan with all the tales about Sinbad and Aladdin, and those three frisky sisters. Book's called *A Thousand and One Nights*. You ever read anything *not* written by your nutty cousin?"

"Oh, I'm familiar with the story. The name just escaped me. So you told him similar fantastic tales?"

"No. I give it a new angle, see? I figure, him bein' a typical male of the species, and a pirate besides, he wouldn't like hearin' *my* tales half so much as talkin' about himself. And boy, did he lay it on thick. You know, he says he won the Battle of New Orleans almost single-handed. Says Andy Jackson only showed up after it was in the bag. I told him that was pretty amazin', since that was more than a hundred years ago."

"How'd he explain that?"

"Didn't. Just poured it on even thicker. Says he fired the gun that killed Admiral Nelson at Trafalgar. And sent the first harpoon into Ahab's white whale. Ferried Washington across the Delaware. Showed Scott the back way into Veracruz, and Dewey into Manila."

"A bit of a blowhard?"

"Bit of a blowhard? Serves nothing but tripe, three meals a day. He's a monger of air, a flying jib, a flashman of fables, a knight first class of the fertilizer fork.... Spends more time peddling piffle than piratin'."

"Or ravishing women, from the sounds of it. Sesbania

concluded the Lafittes and their crew prefer the company of men. Maybe that accounts for Jean's... passivity?"

She blushed, and her tone became prickly. "Told you that, did she?" I doubt there are many women who'd be embarrassed at not having been ravished by a blood-thirsty pirate, but Aggie, apparently, was one. "Well, I got some secrets I could share, too."

"If you mean that she's not really Sesbania, I know that."

"Do ya? And do ya know she's nothin' but the whore-wife of a one-eyed rum-runner named La Baza?"

"No, she hadn't mentioned that."

"And that I put her up to playin' your not-wife?"

"*You* put her up to it? But how'd you even know this girl looked like Sesbania?"

"Took a snapshot from your hotel room in Pensacola, the two of you in Paris. Guess you didn't notice it missing. Only picture you had of her. Real sentimental, ain't ya?"

"Thought it'd been mislaid. But how'd you know we weren't married?"

"You said you got hitched in London, last November. I had someone at the bureau there check on it."

"Sounds like a lot of effort. What about my scar?"

"Saw it through the same peephole you probably used to gawk at me—just before pluggin' it up."

"So you described me in detail so she could recognize me.... But what about the moustache? How'd you know Sesbania's attitude toward facial hair?"

"Simple. You only started growin' the thing after she got nabbed. So you must have preferred it—but were too... uxorious."

"Uxorious?"

"Sure, uxorious. Din't you take Latin? Means under her thumb, she's put a spell on ya."

I'd forgotten Aggie was Ivy League. It seemed ironic that this was one bit of vocabulary my Latin teacher hadn't mentioned.

"One reaches certain accommodations...," I told her. "Anyway, that's the *how*. But *why* did you do it?"

"Well, that willingness to accommodate got me to wonderin' if maybe you didn't care something for her. So then I see this double among Lafitte's booty. I don't know about you, but I've been seein' doubles everywhere. Like Geoff and Albertson, an' a rum-runner we took off of New Jersey—looked just like my editor...."

"Yes, it's uncanny. As a matter of fact, Jack's the spitting image of Congdon."

"*Congdon?* Can't be much of a pirate then."

"The similarity doesn't run any deeper. Trust me, when he needs to be, Jack's plenty... piratical."

"That a word? Piratical?"

"So I'm told. But getting back to your story, you'd just noticed the girl looked like Sesbania."

"Yeah, I seen her down there in Barataria, and I figure, maybe you'd come by there to see if he had the real one. Or maybe to rescue me. Did you? I mean, come to rescue me?"

"Oh, yes. Ideally, to rescue you both. Jack Tigue and I."

"Anyway, Jean was already plannin' to auction her in St. Pierre, so I prepped her and told her it would be worth her while if she could convince you she was your not-wife. Assumin' you came and bid on her."

"So you were just testing me?"

"I wanted to see if there was anythin' to yer story.

We dropped her off a couple days ahead a' time, then hunted rum-runners 'til the day of the auction. But you beat us to the punch."

"What if I hadn't? Would you have turned me over to Lafitte?"

"He only wanted the booze you'd be biddin' with. I wasn't sure what I was gonna do. By the way, that was some working over you gave the place. Jean's a little perturbed about that."

"So's my father-in-law. We knocked over his bar-room during the same episode."

"You mean Bonnet? What's he like?"

"Rutledge's doppelganger. A Mormon who propagates semi-mythical daughters the way other men do cucumbers."

"When you say semi-mythical, where exactly are ya drawin' the line?"

"Well, physically, they're all girl. But temperamentally, they hew pretty closely to their mythical mandates. Sloth is as Sloth does, of course. Clio's bookish, but very pleasant. The rest can all be challenging. Melpomene's surprisingly cunning; Avarice, Pride, and Envy frequently dangerous; and Wrath.... Well, let's just say you don't want to upset her if she has a sharp object handy."

"Ah, ishkabibble. I can handle a blade as good as anybody!"

"Perhaps... But not any *Sin*. Trust me, you'd be fighting above your weight class."

"So *you* say. But thanks for carin'."

She afforded me a rare little smile. One that wasn't categorically sardonic or derisive—even if it did incorporate elements of both. If I hadn't known better, I would have said she was flirting.

"So whattaya plan ta do now? Go lookin' for your not-wife? Or you content with the ones you got?"

"Well, as it happens, we met the pirates who abducted her from the *Paris*."

"Yeah? Who was it?"

"A band of females. Travel in a big black airship they call *The Midnight Sun*."

"Who's their captain?"

"A woman Clio called Tryphaena, but apparently that's just a nickname. Tall, long black hair, a certain viciousness about the mouth. Doesn't look like anyone I know. They stopped by and checked Sesbania's bum, then left."

"Checked her bum?"

"She has a mole on the left cheek. The substitute has it on the right."

"So you figure the Amazons kidnapped your not-wife and then lost her somehow?"

"Yes. One of their warriors defected and I'm hoping to interview her as soon as it seems safe."

"As soon as it seems safe?"

"Her defection was incomplete. She hasn't quite gotten around to accepting my authority."

"Who has?"

"Point taken. Nevertheless, last time I encountered her, she gave some indication of wanting to take my head off."

II

As it happened, that very afternoon Antiope came looking for me.

"Percival an' me wanna get hitched—as in married."

"Delightful news," I told her. "May I be the first to congratulate you. I'm sure you'll find every happiness together." Frankly, I was surprised he'd survived that first night with her.

"*You ain't gettin' it.*" Her unique voice had jumped an octave and now fell just short of pain-inducing. "We want *you* ta marry us. You bein' the captain."

"Well, that's sort of a myth."

"*What?*"

"The idea that a captain of a ship has authority to marry people." Once again, that wild-eyed look came over her and I rethought my reply. "I'd love to. Whenever it's convenient."

"*Now* it's convenient. Only, you gotta come upstairs cuz Percival says he's too busy to come down here. Be there in ten minutes."

I agreed, and on the way picked up Aggie to act as a witness.

"I'm hoping her joy in the occasion will soften her up for a chat regarding Sesbania's whereabouts…. But it will take plenty of softening up."

"Tough broad?"

"The very definition of piratical."

On our approach, Antiope summoned her betrothed and the pair of them stood before me arm in arm. And what a pair they were. Her pirate costume looked even more raggedy than it had a couple days before—and her person a few degrees more filthy. I took it she'd been helping Percival with the plumbing. He was a short fellow, balding, dressed in overalls, and wearing heavy-framed eyeglasses. In his right hand, he held her left, and in his left, a greasy monkey wrench.

I remembered a few key phrases, and recited those

in whatever order they came to me. Then they exchanged brass washers in lieu of rings.

"You may now kiss the bride," I told the groom.

But it was Antiope who sprang on him. For a moment, it looked as if she planned to consummate the thing with us as witnesses, much as they're said to have done in medieval times.

"Hey," Aggie whispered. "Don't you recognize her?"

"Her? I think I can say with some certainty, I've never set eyes on her before."

"You wash her up, and *that's* Liz Rutledge."

"You sure? Her father showed me a photo and I don't remember her looking anything like that."

"Well, I ain't sayin' it would be a quick wash-up, but that's her all right. There ain't no mistakin' that voice. Anyway, we can test the hypothesis easy enough." She went over to where the bride was helping her husband from the floor. "Congrats, Lizzie."

Once more, the eyes went wild—but this time only briefly. Aggie had hit the piratical nail on its head.

"Why ya callin' me that?"

"Come on, don't ya remember? I interviewed you the night of your debutante ball."

She thought a moment before replying. "My father send ya?"

"Not me. Him." She pointed a thumb in my direction.

"You? *Well, I ain't goin' back!*"

"That's OK with me," I assured her. "I effectively terminated my relationship with your father before we left. But there are some questions I'd like to ask."

"Questions? You go back to work, precious," she told Percival. "I need to talk to these people."

Her groom seemed curiously uninterested in the

conversation and went off without further prompting.

"Come on." She led us to some crates they'd been using as a makeshift dining room set. "Would you like some coffee?"

She was speaking now like a proper young lady—though it must be admitted, a proper young lady with a very irritating voice. She poured the coffee, then sat down opposite us.

"What is it you want to know?"

"Well, I suppose you're aware that my wife was abducted at the same time you were, back on the *Paris*."

"Oh, sure. Sesbania—Orithyia now."

"Orithyia?"

"A *nom de guerre,* like Antiope."

"*Nom de guerre*?"

"Well, *nom de* pirate, I guess."

"So the abduction was a sort of recruitment?"

"Yes—more or less."

"And you all went along with it?"

"Oh, not all. Only five of us agreed to sign articles and stay aboard the *Sun*."

"And the rest?" Aggie asked.

"Well, they were given their choice. Go back to where they came from, or be put down in alternate New York. They all chose to stay on this side. Seemed like too much fun to pass up, getting away from parents, and husbands."

"Then these pirates can go back and forth between worlds at will?"

"*Could.* I don't know how—it was kept a big secret. But apparently there's been some sort of malfunction."

"And so after signing articles, you've been cruising around with these pirates? Attacking other ships?"

"Rum-runners, mostly. But we do occasional recruitments. That's how we lost Orithyia."

"Lost how?"

"You ever hear of a pirate named Jack Tigue? He also travels with a harem."

"Yes, we've met. You attacked him, hoping to set free his harem?"

"That was the idea. See, our captain, Marpesia, has a real grudge against him and his whole gallantry act. She feels it just perpetuates the idea women are weak creatures in need of a man's protection."

"She's right," Aggie interjected.

"Yeah, I suppose. Anyway, we disabled Tigue's ship and Orithyia led the initial wave of the boarding party. Only he tricked us. He wasn't really disabled. He had a way to clean off our fudge."

"Fudge?"

"The concoction we use to disable enemy vessels. More like caramel, really. You shoot it on hot and it hardens in seconds. Just as you found out, the only way to get it off is with steam. Well, he was already set up for that. So he took off with Orithyia and six others still aboard. Then a week later, we heard a rumor Lafitte had Orithyia and was taking her to St. Pierre to be auctioned. But by the time we got there, you'd taken her. Of course, now I know she wasn't the real Orithyia."

"But assuming she had been, didn't it seem reasonable for me, her husband, to take her with me?"

"She told us she wasn't keen on going back to you."

"Any particular reason?"

"No, we didn't ask for details. Anyway, the captain had developed a liking for Orithyia...."

"How do ya mean, liking?" Aggie asked.

"Well..." Liz answered with an inscrutable smile and slightly raised eyebrows.

"Oh."

"So the night you were abducted, the purpose of the perfume..." I had some difficulty wording my query. "They had plans for you?"

"Well, let's say options were presented. Some availed themselves, some didn't. I chose not to—for the time being. My abductress had dropped her handkerchief which carried the scent and so my choice was made easier. Others got rather caught up in the... well, frenzy."

"Frenzy?"

"Perhaps that's too strong a word. But I think I'll say no more on that subject. I'm a tell-no-tales sort of girl. No hanging dirty linen in public for me."

An odd statement from a young woman dressed in a soiled pirate costume and with one of her breasts still fully exposed. Her thinking apparently ran similarly. She made a vain attempt to button her bodice, then simply held it closed with one of her hands.

"So, as far as you know, Sesbania is still aboard Jack's airship?"

"As far as I know. Marpesia told us at the time they'd probably all be put to the sword. But she tends toward the dramatic.... I wish I had something more promising to tell you."

"Well, thank you. It's much more than I did know."

"Maybe too much," Aggie couldn't help adding.

"This is actually a big relief for me," Liz went on. "You have no idea how exhausting acting pirate is. I can hardly wait to take a hot bath and wash my hair."

I took the vial of perfume from my shoe and handed it to her.

"For your wedding night. I believe you still have one more coming to you."

She blushed—and the pirate girl Antiope vanished before our eyes.

As Aggie and I climbed back down, she stopped me. "What was that you gave her?"

"The perfume the pirates used. It's a... well, a female aphrodisiac...."

"A female aphrodisiac?"

"Yes.... Of unusual potency."

"Huh." She glanced back over her shoulder.

"Listen, I hope I can count on your discretion.... Some of what she told us might prove embarrassing... taken out of context."

"You kiddin'? Don't I work for the *New York World*? We wrote the book on discretion."

It was a bad joke, made even less funny when the damned parrot flew down and landed on her shoulder.

"*We wrote the book on discretion.*"

"You still aboard?" she asked it. "Surprised you ain't been et." The animal squawked. "Come on, I'll get you a cracker."

"*I'm a tell-no-tales sort of girl....*"

Between the bird and his yellow journalist protector, no one on or off the ship—and in either realm, real or fictional—was likely to miss the report of the girls on the S.S. *Paris* being kidnapped by an Amazon press-gang.

III

That evening, we had the first meal prepared by our French kitchen staff. They called it a salmagundi, and said it incorporated everything in the stores worth bothering with. As usual, the Sins and Muses ate in the harem, and the rest of us in the increasingly crowded mess.

The two chefs spent most of dinner muttering their mortification at the inadequacies of the galley and its pantry. The lack of a proper wine cellar they found inconceivable. They shouted, threatened, even displayed cutlery. All very unpleasant—but once you've spent time in the company of Mortal Sins, the indignation of a couple chefs, even French chefs, is quite bearable.

Afterward, I went looking for faux Sesbania. For some reason, she'd skipped the meal and that struck me as odd. Until then, she'd seemed rather fond of her grub. When I found she wasn't in the cabin, it occurred to me she might have gone to the library. Clio had been actively soliciting patrons for days by then.

I didn't find Sesbania there, but the librarian greeted me with a smile. She was the one person on board I could speak freely with. And given the day's revelations, I felt in need of talking. I told her about Aggie's machinations regarding the faux Sesbania, and then Liz's account regarding the real one—or most of it, anyway.

"So she's a phony after all…. But if you couldn't tell the difference, does it really matter? Surely you can't send her back to Caliban."

"Caliban?"

"Well, figuratively. La Baza, also known as *el Cíclope de pelo naranja*."

"How's that?"

"A sobriquet, Spanish for the orange-haired Cyclops. He's a ravening monster, just like the one Odysseus encountered."

"Wow. Some girls really shouldn't be allowed to pick their men."

"I doubt she picked him. He probably charmed her with gifts. He's fabulously wealthy, they say. Then, once he had her in his power..."

"Well, it goes without saying I wouldn't send her back. But that begs the question of how to proceed in regard to her real counterpart."

"The wife who's not your wife?"

"Yes, her. I sincerely doubt Jack put her to the sword. He's generally a conservator of women."

"So I've heard. A harem as large as your own. You think he ravished her and added her to the line-up?"

"That's not really Jack's technique. Any ravishment is by mutual consent."

"Doesn't sound very..."

"I think the word you're looking for is piratical."

"Is it? Too bad—I'd hoped to coin a new one, maybe pyratanical. With a Y following the P to emphasize their fiery disposition. Can you have ravishment by mutual consent?"

"Well..."

"Never mind. But tell me this: does your Sesbania run so fickle you need to worry about Jack Tigue?"

"Sesbania's not fickle. Or, at least, not last I saw her. But I think she may be..."

"Sowing her oats?"

"Yes, exactly."

"I heard about her and Tryphaena, or Marpesia, as she calls herself."

"Oh. So you've spoken with Liz?"

"Liz?"

"The former Antiope. Her role as Liz Rutledge actually predates the pirate performance. I wonder if we should start a roster with all the aliases. They're really starting to pile up."

"No, not her. The parrot's been talking again."

"You don't happen to have any manuals on the poisoning of birds, do you?"

"No, sorry. But the news shouldn't have come as a shock—I told you she was a seeker of pleasure."

"Yes, but Sesbania's never displayed any predilections in that direction before."

"*That you know of.* Tell me, did she go to boarding school?"

"No. But she did attend a women's college."

"Enough said.... While we're on the subject of ravishment, I hear I missed my chance."

"Missed your chance?"

"To avoid being last on the list. Pride and Wrath snuck in ahead of me."

"Oh.... Well, that was rather spur of the moment.... Did I mention the perfume the Amazons use to subdue their captives? *Deux nuits d'excès,* it's called."

"Two nights of excess? Sounds hyperbolic."

"You'd think so, wouldn't you?" I gave her a general picture of the drug's effect on her sisters and the two Sesbanias and she seemed impressed. "I gave it back to Liz, for her wedding night, otherwise I could treat you to some now. I mean, if you were so disposed...."

"Oh, I'm so disposed. Auntie Selene has come and gone, and it's about time we sealed the bargain. Where will you have me?"

"Ah..."

"How about here?" She doffed her robe and hopped onto an upended crate holding an open book. It didn't look particularly comfortable, but she was devoted to her collection. I kissed and petted and she did likewise with apparent enthusiasm. Then I knelt down and gave her the patented treatment. She seemed to have been expecting it, based on the reports of either her sisters or the parrot. There must have been some volumes on anatomy in her collection, because she had a very keen understanding of her own. Much like my old Latin teacher, she gave me very specific instructions.

I suppose some might find compass directions less than arousing, especially when they're given not just in degrees, but in minutes and seconds as well. I personally appreciate the help. There's a job to be done and it may as well be done right.

However, her precision led me to believe her knowledge was of too personal a nature to have been derived solely from books, or even navigational manuals. Perhaps, like Envy, she'd shared a bed with Lust as a child. Anyway, outside of the course data, she didn't say much beyond a scattering of moans and a handful of "ohs!". But whenever I hit the target, she'd shiver quite noticeably, and the beads in her hair would make a sibilant sound like a baby's rattle given a half-shake.

The endgame, however, didn't go off quite as planned. I was checkmated by a sharp blow to the head.

By that time in my adventure, I'd received an embarrassment of blows to the head, a bumper crop of swollen lumps, and a veritable cavalcade of concussions. Yet this one stood out, both for its speedy effect and for the prolonged headache which followed.

I awoke on the floor, naked and hog-tied. In all honesty, it would be difficult to accurately assign the cause of my throbbing head, as Melpomene was back at the calliope, lamenting. When weighed against that, a blow to the head might well be seen as a blessing.

The merciless itching, however, I quite easily attributed to the mystery vine lining the path by which Aggie had led us out of Barataria. I've had a long association with poison ivy, and knew its incubation period to be something on the order of twenty-four hours. I also knew it would get worse before it got better. Much worse.

My torments occupied a good part of my thoughts that morning, but not to the exclusion of all else. For instance, with the sun poking directly through a starboard porthole, I estimated the time at about nine. And the absence of the customary chugga-chugga of the steam engines led me to conclude we'd made port somewhere.

Not long after, Aggie came upon me.

"*Jeez-us*. What'd they do, take a switch to you?"

She applied her razor to the rope binding my wrists and ankles.

"If you mean the welts, it's poison ivy. From that shortcut you led us down. I'm surprised you aren't showing signs—the way you crawled around in it looking for your thumb."

"Never get it." She pulled a sheet off of Clio's makeshift daybed and handed it to me. "Cover yourself up, it's too depressin' to look at.... I figured they had you tied up somewhere."

"Who's they?"

"Near everyone! You had a regular mutiny. The cooks, the wives—save Cassandra up at the steam organ and little Miss Greedy-Two-Shoes."

"What about Horatio?"

"Well, he didn't go with 'em—but didn't try to stop 'em either. Just put a finger up to the wind."

"So the others have abandoned the ship?"

"Just for the time bein'. They went into Havana. On some sort of shopping spree. They figured you and Avarice might object, so they locked her in her money chest and knocked you out *in flagrante*. Who with?"

"Well..."

"Never mind."

"What about you?"

"Me? It was no skin off my nose."

"And Sesbania?"

"You mean the fake? Must have slept through it."

I went over to one of the few remaining crates of rum dressed as Scotch and opened a bottle. I took a long slug, then handed it to Aggie.

"What the hell," she said. "Never got breakfast."

After we'd put a healthy dent in the bottle, she offered to go by my cabin and fetch some clothes for me. "Pink ain't your color."

Once she'd gone, I took another long slug. It didn't do much to deaden the pain, but there were two more cases available. The knowledge that Clio could be as devious as her sisters had left me feeling friendless. One expects that sort of behavior from a Mortal Sin. But aren't the Muses billed as benign?

Aggie returned with my duds and waited while I dressed.

"Gave *her* something to think about," she said.

"Who?"

"The rum-runner's whore-wife. Told her you woke up with nothin' to wear. Then let her come to her own conclusion."

"Why didn't you just tell her I'd been sandbagged? It's the truth."

"*Jeezus.* I can't believe them words came outta your mouth. Only truth you know is the one that serves your purpose."

I was well used to her cynicism, but her tone this time sounded more peevish than skeptical. Quite unexpectedly, she offered to escort me back to my cabin.

Sesbania was out. While I got into bed, Aggie went and fetched some moist cloths, then carefully placed them over the worst of my welts.

She was one strange sheba, all right.

CHAPTER 5.

THE TORTUGA TWO-STEP

No sooner had Aggie left my cabin than Avarice arrived. She, at least, was her normal self.

"What's this lying in bed? We need to get under way—*now!*"

"Have your sisters gotten back?"

"No—and if you move fast, we'll be long gone before they do. The little sneaks stole my hoard!"

She picked up the brandy decanter and flung it at the wall; the shattered glass ricocheted about the cabin. The very next moment, her body went limp and she slumped onto the edge of the bed, spent. Then, much to my amazement, actual tears emerged from the corners of her eyes. She bit her lip to keep from crying. But despite her efforts, her chest began heaving.

Had her sisters' treachery cut her so deeply? Were these the tears of a familial love betrayed? Do even Sins have souls?

"The filthy pagans! Didn't leave me more than a few hundred francs. If I ever catch sight of them again, *I'll gnaw out their hearts!*"

Apparently not.

My own feelings were running similar to hers. (Though I doubt I could ever work myself up to the extracting of organs by tooth and jaw alone. Far too much work, if nothing else.) Leaving before her sisters returned would free me from a good deal of potential trouble: four Mortal Sins and an untrustworthy Muse. I only regretted they hadn't taken Melpomene on their expedition—she was still at the calliope, and still *very* unhappy.

The French cooking would be missed, but not the prerequisite Gallic cheek. Of insolence, I'd had a surfeit. Since taking command in Pensacola, it seemed I'd fed on nothing but. By then, I'd lost count of the mutinies, near-mutinies, and miscellaneous acts of insubordination.

"All right," I told her. "I'll make preparations."

Her mood brightened. "They'll wet their robes when they see we've abandoned them!" Then she cackled, maniacally. At times like this, it was difficult to remember how seductive she could be.

I found Horatio and Albertson in the mess having coffee with their respective consorts.

"Prepare to get under way," I told them.

"Leave behind them wives of yours?" Horatio asked. "Ain't abandonment a prosecutable offense?"

"So is polygamy. Besides, we're privateers—we have a mandate from on high: Calvin Coolidge himself."

"Who's he?"

I'd forgotten Silent Cal didn't exist in Cousin Emmie's world. One had to credit her for at least one change for the better.

"Never mind. Just get ready to shove off. Albertson, prepare to take up the lines."

"He ain't finished his cake yet!" Dottie interjected.

"Well, eat quick. We sail at noon."

In fact, we beat that time—just not according to my plan. It was twenty of the hour when the away party arrived in a commandeered wagon and loaded their plunder at breakneck speed. Just as they finished, the cause of their frenzy appeared in the guise of a small but very energetic troop of Cuban cavalry. As we lifted off, one of their number managed to grab onto a line. Unfortunately for him, he'd chosen the one Wrath was being winched up on. She shimmied back down to greet him. At least we can be sure he died quickly.

Mercifully for us all, her sisters made an effort to soothe the aggrieved Greed. The balm coming in the form of jewelry, sweets, and her favorite tobacco, a truly repulsive blend of the foulest shags. She remained livid with rage. But for the moment at least, she set aside ideas of gnawing at their flesh.

The cooks stuffed their larder with choice meats, cheeses, and fresh produce. Strings of sausages were hung all about the galley and mess. Clio came aboard with a canvas satchel crammed full. Before she disappeared, our eyes met briefly. Embarrassed, she smiled tentatively and shrugged. Why is it women think a shrug the universal rationalization?

Even more surprising than her duplicity was the energy displayed by Sloth. Her share of the goods consisted of bundles of what looked like woven rope. Later, when she'd had a chance to deploy them, we saw they comprised a dozen hammocks. She distributed them strategically about the ship, ensuring she'd never need to venture more than twenty yards if she found herself in sudden need of a nap.

As soon as we were under way, I set course for Tortuga. I still harbored some hope Avarice could be persuaded to skip this stop. But given the timing, it would have to be handled gingerly. Sins are rather slow to recover from their losses, and she missed her money dearly. More dearly than you or I can imagine.

About ten that evening, my opportunity arrived. She summoned me to her lair. The air was thick with her tobacco, and I sat on a pillow to be as far below the cloud as possible.

"When will we reach Tortuga?"

"Not until about ten in the morning."

"Well, we'll just have to wait until tomorrow night then."

"I don't know if I mentioned it before, but I had a somewhat negative experience with Clarisse when we last met."

"Oh? Did she have you to dinner?"

By her smile, I realized I'd been wrong to think she was ignorant of Clarisse's eating habits.

"She did, yes. But when we parted, it wasn't on the best of terms."

"I've heard she's a hard woman to satisfy—though Smedley always seems to get on well with her.... Didn't she mistake you for him?"

"There were some clues that she did, but at the time I wasn't aware of his existence. Anyway, I'm not sure our plan will work as well given her feelings toward me."

"Who knows, maybe she'll give you another chance to come through? ...Perhaps a little preparation is in order. After all, practice makes perfect."

She sat just as she had on my last visit: sprawled on her couch, her robe loose about her. This time, there wasn't the slightest chance of misinterpreting her intent. Nor did I feel inclined to pass on the offer. She was, when she wanted to be, the most arousing of all my wives. And from her sultry pose, I took it she wanted to be. Her eyes alone, their lovely hazel partly veiled by languid lids, were enough to bring me to my knees. Which they shortly did.

As expected, the session provided a welcome distraction from my painful rashes, which were now at their worst. And I believe it afforded her some slight diversion from her overriding concern as well. She once again sang the praises of accumulating large quantities of swag. But instead of dull calculations—accruing interest, returns on principal, etc.—it came as breathless expostulations. "Oh, think, think of it! More money than we could ever have conceived! Piles and piles.... *A little higher....* We'll fill treasure rooms with gold and silver! *No, you've lost your place, back to the left a little....*"

Seeing that I shared her enthusiasm for the subject of her monologue, her cries only fueled my eagerness to please—while her asides gave useful intimations as to how to go about it. I would estimate I was at it almost as long as our first session together. But this time, I didn't flag. And neither did I wait for some decisive conclusion on her part. Her yens were physiologically incapable of satisfaction.

When I felt it time, I rose and fell upon her. And she accepted me eagerly. From the bites on my neck, I might even say hungrily. One way or another, I suppose, she'd have her meal of flesh....

We breakfasted in bed the next morning, but only after another long workout. She struck a fairly business-like attitude toward the sex itself. A little cold, perhaps, but an improvement over the one-sided transaction of a week earlier. This time, I received payment in kind.

More unexpected were the one or two moments when her voice took on a hint of sentimentality. Only briefly, and it may be I mistook breathless exhaustion for hesitant emotion. Still, something had changed. Perhaps the action of her sisters had awoken her conscience, and given her a new self-awareness—or, perhaps, simply a more formidable libido.

Under the impression we'd set aside lovemaking for

food, I'd been partaking of a croissant when she quite suddenly flung it from my hand and pounced on me. In doing so, she splayed me diagonally across the bed, with my head hanging over the edge. While she licked my wounds, and such, I caught sight of two pairs of eyes peeking from the drapery. One pair belonged definitely to Pride, the red bangs giving her away. The other pair was about a foot lower down. These eyes had a dangerously resentful look about them; they could only have belonged to Envy.

Whether Avarice had only just noticed them, or the entire night had been for their benefit, and this a mere encore, I couldn't say. But one thing was sure: she was deliberately provoking them as payback for their betrayal. Of course, there was little doubt yours truly would ultimately bear the brunt of it. Above each pair of eyes was a furrowed brow—in Pride's case, it needed to be inferred beneath her bangs, but it was there, all right.

As any spouse of women knows, a furrowed brow is a warning. Displayed by a Sin, it may be taken as a storm flag. And when you see one above another, a hurricane is imminent. To mitigate the provocation, I tried not to exhibit too much satisfaction with Avarice's ministering below deck. But that just seemed to drive her to greater application. And she was a girl of grit and determination. Not to mention flair and imagination.

The paroxysms had only just subsided when someone flung open the curtain.

II

"Sorry ta intrude, but I figured you'd want to know. We're over Tortuga now." It was Aggie. Behind her, I could see the two voyeurs sneaking off. "Though it looks like you already made port."

"What's the matter, dear—no one willing to tie up at your berth?" the greedy one asked. "Perhaps the crustaceans skittering about your quay put them off?"

When it comes to catty, not even the jaded newspaperwoman is a match for the acerbic Sin. Aggie seemed to sense this. After making a vain attempt at face-saving with a contemptuous snarl, she went on her way.

I was dressing when Horatio arrived to repeat the news Aggie had already announced.

"Let's try to moor a little closer to town than last time," I told him. "We may need to get away from here quickly."

"No late supper with Clarisse?" he asked with his usual impertinence. The mocking tone, however, struck me as new.

"Depends on what she's serving. Now see to the mooring."

"Aye, aye, sir."

I turned to say good-bye to Avarice, but she was sleeping like a baby. Well, a greedy, plotting baby.

On my way out of the labyrinth, I came upon Clio.

"I want you to know, it wasn't my idea. Knocking you out like that. But we'd made a compact."

"A compact?"

"If you visited any of us that evening, we'd do our best to distract you."

"Why didn't you just say what you had in mind?"

"Well, we knew Avarice would be against stopping, and you seemed in league with her.... Even more than we suspected, apparently."

News travels fast in a harem.

"What was it you were shopping for?"

"Books! I talked Pride and Wrath into a raid on the Biblioteca Nacional. The rare book room. We now have a thirteenth-century manuscript of the *Disciplina clericalis*."

"Do we, indeed? ...What's that?"

"A book of exempla by a Spanish monk named Petrus Alphonsi, a Moorish convert. It's a collection of fables and aphorisms meant to provide instruction, many taken from Arabic sources, others coming from elsewhere in the East. You can be sure it was on Chaucer's reading list, and Boccaccio's. I'm thinking of translating it into English."

"Well, just so my bludgeoning wasn't for nothing."

"Oh, certainly not. I acquired a number of other items of interest, as well. But I've only just begun the cataloguing."

"Was it your raid that brought the cavalry out?"

"Yes. But as Father is so fond of saying, a skirmish is the unavoidable consequence of book collecting."

"*Piratical* book collecting."

"Is there another sort?"

"None so economical, I'm sure."

She smiled, then went on her way.

I didn't think it a good idea to meet Sesbania in my current state, so I stopped on the way to shower. But this time, a cold shower—hot water aggravated the itching.

By the time I arrived in the control room, the ship had been moored and the crew was absent. I could hear them in the mess enjoying their lunch. Sesbania must have been there too, as the cabin was empty. I seized the opportunity to lie down and take a nap. I had a lot of catching up to do, and I slept soundly—right up to the moment the door of the cabin was kicked violently open.

Jack entered with his cutlass drawn and the general aspect of a pirate vexed. I don't mind admitting, his attitude concerned me. I'd seen him in a similar pose just prior to eviscerating several of the Lafittes' men.

"Where is she?"

"I suspect you're referring to Miss Biddle."

"Who else?"

"Well, I'm afraid she's been mislaid...." My words were ill chosen, and not only due to the unintentional rhyme. There was a palpable rise in the level of menace. "I didn't lay a finger on her, Jack. We were both prisoners of the Lafittes and attempted to escape together. I set her aside for a moment, in order to create a diversion, and when I returned, she was gone...."

"Set her aside where?"

"The walk-in cooler, in the kitchen there."

"You jackass! I came by the next morning. If you'd left her alone, I'd 'a gotten her away without a hitch."

"No doubt, Jack. But how was I to know that?"

"Get dressed. Then ya can tell me what ya *do* know."

I dressed as quickly as possible, then led his party of three to the mess, where I had coffee and pastries served. With time, Jack's anger abated. It seemed he had a penchant for a good éclair, and luckily, Reynard had a penchant for making them.

I gave him as complete an account as I could of my time with his young friend. But he wasn't yet convinced of my innocence.

"Lafitte says she left with you."

"If she had, why on earth would I keep it a secret from you? Couldn't he have found her and merely stashed her somewhere else in the house?"

"Wasn't much left of the house when I was through lookin'."

"Well, if he doesn't have her, she must have snuck out and gotten a ride with another ship. She told me she'd been hitchhiking when Lafitte picked her up."

"Hitchhiking in pirate ports... talk about a babe in the woods...."

"Now that I've told you what I know about her, I wonder if I might ask you about something concerning me."

"Your wife, you mean."

"Yes. I understand she boarded your ship—with aggressive intent. I hope she didn't create any inconvenience...."

"They gave up pretty quick when they saw they were cut off. Then she tried to talk my girls into a mutiny."

"A mutiny? Any luck?"

"Fat chance. I'll never get rid of them that easy. Anyway, when she realized that was no go, we came to terms."

"Came to terms?"

"By the way, Celia sends her regards."

That, apparently, was the only elaboration I'd be receiving.

"Is she still aboard the *Goose*?"

"Celia? Sure."

"I meant my wife."

"Oh. So far as I know."

"No she ain't," one of his crew corrected. "Saw her sneak off sometime 'round noon. Then later, I saw her goin' aboard a tramp steamer."

"A boat?" I asked.

"Yeah."

"Any idea where it was bound?"

"Nah. But it was *The Slippery Eel* she boarded."

"Talk about chancy...," Jack opined.

"You know the boat?"

"Never heard of it. But I wouldn't want any wife of mine travelin' on a tub called *The Slippery Eel*."

"I suppose I could find out from the harbor master where it's bound."

"*Harbor master?* In a pirate port?"

"Well, then I'll just ask about the docks."

"Go about the docks asking questions like that, and you'll be floating out with the tide. I'll find out and let you know. How long are you here for?"

"Through tonight. Probably leave early morning."

"Ain't ya gonna introduce me?"

Aggie had arrived. I made the introductions and she sat down.

"Never read newspapers, myself," Jack told her.

"That's all right. I don't peddle 'em. My end's gettin' the story. An' I figure you're worth a few of 'em."

"Maybe. But why should I give 'em up to you? Maybe I'd rather tell 'em myself."

"You serious?"

"Why not?"

"Well, if ya are, I could help ya there."

"You mean, be my official biographer?"

"Sure. Why not?"

"Well, the job's open. Last one didn't make it past chapter one."

"What happened?"

"Asked too many questions."

"Well, maybe I'll ask nicer."

"I bet you will.... All right, get your things."

I wasn't sure if Jack had made yet another effortless conquest, or Aggie had. Either way, they left a little later still bantering—and without bothering to say good-bye.

I drank a good deal that evening, partly to deaden the incessant itching, but principally to steel my resolve. For me, courage has almost always come by way of a bottle. Some might call it mere delusion. But to me the two have always seemed interchangeable.

We left the ship about eleven, hoping to arrive at the Pelican before Clarisse sat down for her evening meal. We were taken to a back room off the bar and there waited a good hour before our hostess arrived, only moderately disheveled. Perhaps she'd been nibbling hors d'oeuvres.

She was suspicious right from the start. Avarice had anticipated this and told her that on the last occasion, she'd hosted an impostor.

"Did he have a moustache?" the Sin asked.

"Yes. A little raggedy one."

"The bastard's been masquerading as Smedley here for months! Hasn't he?"

"Yes," I agreed. "A little unnerving, having a double out there."

"Well, if it's any consolation," Clarisse told me, "he could only carry off the impersonation from the neck up." She laid a shapely calf on my lap, and with it, massaged me to attention.

Avarice bit her lip. She found my discomfort amusing.

Our hostess had her money box brought to her and Avarice went about divvying its contents into the three allotments—one for future operations, Clarisse's share, and ours.

"If you two want to go off and have a bite, I can manage here," Avarice told us.

It seemed odd that my lover of a scant twelve hours before was now acting my procuress. Odder still when you consider she was also my wife. I'd clearly been mistaken when I thought I'd seen hints of sentiment during our time in bed. There was only one thing she was sentimental about and there were three equal piles of it before her.

Were the barkeep to take me upstairs, Avarice could make a clean getaway. What would happen to me after that didn't concern her. Clarisse, fortunately—or not, depending on your point of view—was anything but gullible.

"Better we wait until we're *ravenous,*" she said. "Don't you think?"

I smiled enigmatically. If she didn't let up with the calf soon, she was going to be once more disappointed. She'd had a concoction of rum, fruit juice, and crushed ice served and I took the opportunity to spill mine in my lap. That only bought me about five minutes—her leg never moved. She kept right on with the massage until a footman poked his head in.

"Jack has come to say good-bye. He's waiting upstairs."

"*Jack!*" she said, rising hypnotically. Then she ran from the room without so much as a backward glance.

Avarice looked at me inquisitively. "Someday I'll have to meet this Jack Tigue. What is it about him?"

"You're asking the wrong person."

I doubt she heard my answer, or even cared by then. She was shoveling the money into the leather bag we'd brought along.

We left via a rear window and raced back to *Lucy.*

"How much did we get?" I asked.

"Not as much as we should have. She spends so damn much on glassware the profits get eaten up before the month's out."

III

We reached the ship about two that morning. As soon as we boarded, Avarice went off to replenish her money chest.

"Jack sent you a note," Horatio told me, then read it out loud: "*Slippery Eel* sailed for Mayagüez at three."

"Good. They won't get there before noon tomorrow," I said. "If we get under way now, we'll beat them by hours."

"Whatta we want with slippery eels?"

"It seems my wife boarded that boat."

"Which wife? If you mean Sesbania, she's waitin' for you in there." He waved a thumb at my cabin door.

"There's something I haven't told you. Sesbania, the one waiting in there, isn't my wife. Just her mirror image. My Sesbania—the real one—was taken prisoner by Jack. The day he was attacked by *The Midnight Sun*."

"The day you run away and left him to fend for himself?"

"Well, if you want to take the uncharitable view. Anyhow, today she left his ship and boarded *The Slippery Eel*. By the way, where were you when Jack stopped by?"

"Well, when he comes aboard and says, 'Where's that goddam captain of yours? I'm gonna carve him into chops!', I figure maybe it's a good time to go up and oil the engines. Albertson too."

"I've never noticed Albertson in need of lubricant."

"Listen, I don't get paid enough to play straight man.... So your wife's gone off fishin' for eels, and Aggie's run out on you. Brings you down to eight, by my count."

"Aggie's definitely not mine. I don't know what gave you the idea she was."

"Oh, little things. But maybe I was dreamin' 'em."

"Well, try to rouse yourself and make way east by southeast. I'll give you the precise course as soon as I change."

"Yeah," he said, looking at my lap. "Looks like you had an accident."

"Just get going and save the commentary."

"Aye, aye, sir."

Faux Sesbania was lying awake in bed, reading my logbook. It'd been days since I'd written in it.

"There you are," she said. She snapped the book shut and tossed it on the desk. "I was worried I'd seen the last of you...."

"Why'd you think that?"

"The last two nights, you never came in.... All I can say is, I'm sorry. It was a horrid thing to do! Taking advantage of your love for your wife.... I can't believe I let that woman talk me into it. It was all her idea...."

"Aggie? So she told me. She's a strange specimen, all right. But I actually found out a few days ago. When we were boarded by the Amazon pirate queen. You see, you're *almost* Sesbania's double. The exception being the mole on your bum. Hers is on the left, yours the right."

"Oh... But you have it backwards."

She tossed off the sheet and spun around. She was right. *Hers* was on the left. I'm not sure why I couldn't keep it straight, but I suspected it was due to the fact I often viewed her bum in a mirror, and even when I did approach it directly, as I was doing just then, it was as likely as not from an odd angle.

Over time, that shapely bit of anatomy had come to represent the cozy comforts of home. And given its portability, one that need never be far from hand. Especially now that there were two. I lavished it with wet kisses and more than a few playful bites, taking care to plant the topography firmly in mind so as not to embarrass myself again. Then I went and snuck under her. She rose on her haunches and I performed the work I perform so well. She seemed to think so too.

She couldn't from this position reach the wall to slap it. Instead, she began chanting something that sounded like the ancient Greek spoken by some of Captain Bonnet's wives. Perhaps her former consort, the Cyclops, was part Greek? Real Sesbania never chanted at such times— or any other times, that I'm aware of.

A few minutes into it, she seemed to have found a way to reach the wall, because there were several loud bangs and the chanting came to an abrupt end.

"I think someone's at the door," she whispered.

"Ignore them."

But they were not to be ignored. The door flew open with a crash. It was the mistress of cupidity, and she'd brought along sister Wrath.

"We'd like a word," Avarice announced. "*If it wouldn't be too much of an inconvenience.*"

"I think maybe you should go talk to them."

"Yes, I suppose I should. Well, save my place."

I dressed and met them out in the control room.

"Why the dramatic entry?" I asked.

"I forgot to mention, we need to head to Nassau next."

"Why? What's in Nassau?"

"The Merry Pelican!"

"I take it that's a pelican who hasn't made the acquaintance of a pirate."

"Not so *many* pirates, anyhow. A new addition I'd forgotten about. It's due for its first plucking right about now."

"We can head there after I finish my business in Mayagüez. It seems my wife—"

"Yes, we heard all about that from your first mate here. But what the hell do you need another wife for? You've seven of us, plus her in there."

"True. But Sesbania and I go back a ways...."

"Did it occur to you *she's* lost interest? Maybe because *her* tastes have changed.... From what that parrot's been saying..."

"Yes, yes. I know what the damn bird's been saying. Mere rumors, all of it."

"Then why didn't she come to you in Tortuga? Instead of boarding that boat?"

"Possibly she wasn't aware we were in port."

"Pah! Well, it doesn't matter. We're going to Nassau and that's final."

"Don't listen to her, Horatio," I ordered.

He looked over at Wrath. She was playfully swinging the whip she'd used on me out on the plank. Pride, also in attendance, sat nearby doing her nails—sharpening them, no doubt.

Horatio licked his finger and held it up in the air. "Wind says, Nassau. Sorry, boss. But ain't you got women enough?"

"Feels like that right now. Wake me in a couple hours and I'll relieve you."

"That won't be necessary," Avarice told me. "I'll let you know when you're needed."

Seeing little chance for resistance, I went back to the solace waiting in my cabin. She was sound asleep, and I had little trouble joining her.

As for real Sesbania, she seemed bent on sowing her wild oats—and I'd have to just let her go on planting. Not that I begrudged her. I'd scattered seed aplenty since her disappearance and felt in no position to throw stones. When we eventually met up again—as I still felt sure we would—it would be ask no questions, tell no tales. She could take her secrets to the grave, and I mine.

There was, however, one secret of hers which wouldn't outlive the morning. When Horatio woke me about ten to tell me we'd arrived in Nassau, I found myself alone in bed.

"All right, you go get some sleep," I told him. "By the way, have you seen Sesbania?"

"Done gone."

"Gone? To breakfast?"

"To parts unknown. Soon as we moored, she had me lower her down."

"Why didn't you wake me so I could stop her?"

"She didn't want to be stopped."

"How much did she pay you?"

"Oh, just enough. I ain't greedy."

"Do you have any idea where she was going?"

"To seek out *The Midnight Sun.*"

"She told you that?"

"Told Antiope—I just happened to be there."

"Where is *she?*"

"Said she'd be waitin' for you in the mess."

When I joined her there, Liz had the same look of

commiseration my sister had when she informed me my pet turtle had decamped. (Unlike me, my sister was quite sentimental in her youth. I didn't even remember having a pet turtle.)

"There wasn't anything I could do."

"So... I just spent the night with the real Sesbania, didn't I?"

"Yes. She came aboard yesterday, when everyone was at lunch. I happened upon her when leaving the table. She'd just been in your cabin and found this. It's a letter from her counterpart."

She handed me a page written in a perfect schoolgirl hand. In it, faux Sesbania confessed everything. She said that from my absence the two nights previous, she assumed I was disgusted with her. She didn't deserve me, she said, and would follow where Fate led her.

If she went about boarding tramp steamers with names like *The Slippery Eel*, I didn't imagine Fate would be taking her anywhere good. When I'd finished her letter, Liz handed me a second. I knew at once it was from the real Sesbania because I recognized the barely legible scrawl. It was my own. Her deft work served doubly: to needle me, and to authenticate herself—Sesbania had been forging letters since childhood.

She said she'd been conflicted when she came aboard, unsure what sort of reunion she could expect—or wanted. The seven wives annoyed her, and so did my sleeping with her faux self, but, she said, it wasn't until she heard me give in and abandon her to her fate in Mayagüez that she decided she'd had enough.

"A bit paradoxical," I noted, "given at that time she was right there in the cabin."

"I pointed that out, but she said all that mattered

was what you *thought*. And as you no doubt are aware, she's not easily inclined to cede a point...."

"No, she's not. Well, I guess I better go look for her before she can get too far. Does she have any idea how to find *The Midnight Sun*? Does it stop regularly in Nassau?"

"It didn't while we were aboard. But having been on closer terms with Marpesia, she was probably privy to much I wasn't...."

"Yes, I can imagine...." And I could, too. Quite vividly.

CHAPTER 6.

NASSAU FOR NAUGHT

I suppose I should have been thankful Sesbania had expressed her dissatisfaction via a harmless letter. Whenever she felt herself wronged, reasonableness flew out the window. In fact, my intimate acquaintance with her was the one thing that had prepared me for the Sins. Or, almost so—they, after all, were professionals.

I believe her hypersensitivity originated with the death of her parents. Sesbania'd had an almost indescribably happy childhood. Both mother and father lavished her with love and attention. As did the family friends and servants. Governesses were chosen for their ability to get along with the by then spoiled child.

All that changed, however, when both parents were lost in the *Titanic* disaster. Sesbania, still in her teens, was brought abruptly into the adult world. And she'd never completely recovered from the shock—nor forgiven the world its offense.

Even before her parents' deaths, indignation was something of a hobby for her. Wronged women were a particular concern. I knew this, of course, but I never quite grasped the extent of it until I examined the little chest she traveled with and referred to as her trousseau. It wasn't large, not three feet long and barely one wide, and held little in the way of wardrobe. She never allowed me to get too close a look at its contents, but often I'd come upon her as she was sifting through it. I remember one occasion in particular.

She'd pulled out several items, among them two

wooden forms she insisted were for darning socks. There were two reasons for doubting her. First, she'd never in her life darned a sock. And second, each of these forms came to a rounded point—most unsuitable for darning socks. I suspected they had other uses, and given her obfuscation, I assumed those uses were of an embarrassing, personal nature. But I said no more about it.

Later, after she'd been abducted and the *Paris* made port in New York, I shipped her things to her guardian for safekeeping. Included among these was the chest. Needless to say, I couldn't resist first examining its contents. And ironically, it was Sesbania herself who facilitated my efforts. She'd taught me how to pick locks on our very first outing together.

Mostly, the chest held childhood mementos—the sorts of treasures which have no meaning to anyone but their owner. An old rag doll, a pressed flower, dozens of photographs—and the wooden forms, of course. But one item did arrest my attention. A sealed envelope, addressed thus: *To my dear husband, to be read on the eve of our wedding....*

Another skill Sesbania had shared with me, wisely or not, involved steaming open an envelope without getting it unduly wet.

Inside, I found a thick stack of onionskin. On it, she'd written an account of certain incidents which took place when she was eleven. It was an eventful year, apparently. There was a Bulgarian governess who taught her to forge, and a cook with whom she discussed grisly murders and all things lurid. That, however, was mere prologue.

Just before Christmas that year, her parents traveled to Europe and left her in the care of a family friend she called the countess—the same woman who later became her guardian. This lady was no longer an actual countess, as five years previous her German husband had died—under suspicious circumstances. (Did I mention he was a philanderer? Mere coincidence, they tell me....)

The new count, that man's nephew, was then staying at his step-aunt's house. He was a conceited man, and rather patronizing of little Sesbania. One day he corrected her on a point concerning the lethality of electricity, a subject she'd taken some pains to study. (No, this was *not* your typical eleven-year-old girl.) To cut to the chase, a few days later, the count died in an accidental electrocution—himself thereby giving the lie to his earlier supposition.

How much of the responsibility Sesbania held was left somewhat murky in her account—and intentionally so. But it's fair to say, had she *not* been among the house party that December, the count would have lived to enjoy his Christmas dinner.

Early on in the letter she explains its purpose: she wished to make clear, beyond all doubt, just what she was capable of. A rather chilling read for a groom the evening before his wedding. It's this little tale I was alluding to when I said I should be thankful she'd expressed her dissatisfaction via a note—and not an electric lamp with a frayed cord.

She was a complex girl, all right, a combination of sly ingenuity and unfailing self-assurance. I'd need to work quickly if I was to have any chance of finding her.

The search party consisted of myself, Liz, and the only other members of the company willing to partake, Mattie and Clio—the Muse because she hoped to make amends for her deceit, and Mattie because she was the one person aboard able to empathize with a woman she'd never actually met. Being a native of Nassau, she was also uniquely qualified to help.

Before we left the ship, Liz handed me back the remaining perfume.

"As soon as you come across the much-wronged Orithyia, I suggest you dose her. Only a little left, I'm afraid—I managed to eke four nights out of it."

"I thought two was the limit?"

"So it's said. But I've always run a little hot. And Percival... well..."

"You need say no more."

While Mattie inquired of friends and relatives, Liz, the only one among us familiar with the Amazon crew, would make the rounds of the airship docks. That left Clio and me to canvass the town proper. In order not to draw attention, the Muse exchanged her robe for more typical togs. And I, for much the same reason, donned a slouch hat and a spare pair of Percival's eyeglasses. The disguise was essential. As you may recall, during my earlier visit to Nassau I'd been sentenced to a slow death at sea. My reprieve, purchased with stolen jewels (stolen by, and then from, me), came with the condition that I leave town and never return [Ed. note: see Book One].

Between the hat, the eyeglasses, and my vast compendium of bruises, welts, and rashes, there seemed little likelihood I'd be recognized. I was, however, anything but inconspicuous. Slouch hats were not in vogue in the Nassau of that time. And Percival's powerful lenses rendered everything more than fifteen inches away indistinguishable. In the three hours before lunch, I walked into five lampposts and tipped my hat to no fewer than three merchant seamen. To be fair, these fellows were all slight of build, and, luckily, only the last took offense. His well-placed wallop rendered me briefly unconscious, but it did solve the problem. The lenses were knocked clean out of the eyeglasses, whereupon the affronted tar ground them into dust with his heel.

About two, Clio and I stopped for our midday meal at a pleasant-looking beanery called The Green Parrot. It wasn't particularly ritzy, but there were tablecloths, and ladies present, so doffing the hat was de rigueur. Fortunately, the crowd was thin and the odds seemed against anyone recognizing me.

Not so fortunately, the waiter who came for our order had no trouble doing so. And for good reason. He'd been the night jailer with whom I conspired to gain my release. His recognition didn't come immediately. At first, his interest went no further than my lens-less eyeglasses. He stared at them, moving his head in various directions to sample other views, and then stuck out a finger. Before he could poke me in the eye, I took the things off and handed them to him. He examined them, then turned to Clio and tilted his head in my direction, as if begging an explanation. She held a finger to her lips and he nodded.

This seemed to satisfy him. But on looking back at me, he had a revelation.

"Whatta *you* doin' here?"

"Well, it's a long story. And frankly, I doubt I can remember even half of it. But the essence of it is this: I've lost my wife and she's out roaming around Nassau."

"Well, easy come, easy go." He gave Clio a wink.

"Say, I hope you didn't lose your job at the jail on account of me," I told him.

"Nah. Just fillin' in here. My brother owns the place. Nice, ain't it?"

"Oh, yes. Lovely. By the way, this is Clio, my..." I nearly said it, but she stopped me by once more putting her finger to her lips. Then she finished my sentence for me.

"Egeria."

"*Egeria?*" he asked. "What's that?"

"His adviser—a sage nymph who provides counsel when needed."

"I could use one of those. Got any sisters?"

"Don't ask for trouble," I said.

"Well, I could say the same to you." He lowered his voice. "Yer a wanted man here, ya know. Dead or alive."

"Any reward?" Clio asked.

"If there was, would I be standin' here talkin'?"

"Well, maybe you can help then," I told him. "Ever hear of a pirate airship called *The Midnight Sun*?"

"Doesn't sound familiar—pirates ain't generally welcome here. Unless they behave themselves. And that kinda runs counter to their nature."

"Yes, but these pirates might have an easier time at it: they're all women."

"Oh, yeah. I remember you mentionin' girl pirates. Well, I can't say I've ever seen any. But I'll ask around the kitchen."

He returned at the end of the meal looking decidedly perplexed.

"Did you learn something about the Amazons?"

"Amazons?"

"Girl pirates."

"Oh, nothin' really, only rumors people heard. They say they go about snatching girls of fryin' size and convertin' 'em."

"Oh, dear," Clio said.

"But I picked up a newspaper while waitin for yer grub, an' guess what?"

"What?"

"You was arrested last night."

He handed me the paper, and it was just as he said. I'd been arrested at the well-known watering hole The Merry Pelican. They'd grabbed Smedley by mistake. He protested they had the wrong man, but several witnesses had come forward identifying him—including a former U.S. Navy gob named Burkholtz, and not Brubecker, whom I'd tossed into the drink from forty feet up [Ed. note: Yes, you guessed it, see Book One]. Apparently, the fellow could swim after all.

Clio and I spent the remainder of the afternoon traipsing from one end of town to the other, then returned to the ship only to learn that Mattie had been equally luckless. Liz, however, spoke with a seaman who'd seen someone answering Sesbania's description boarding a smaller airship, *Le Pélican Volant*.

"One of Father's," Clio informed us. "He uses it as a launch. It must have brought Smedley ashore."

"Well, it's gone now," Liz said. "And no one knows where it was headed."

We went directly to the mess on boarding. It was dinner time, and our Gallic chefs refused service to anyone having the effrontery to arrive late at the table. They'd been to the fish market and we had three sumptuous courses of fresh seafood as a result. The only blemish on the meal being their near-constant bickering. Since the Frenchmen's arrival, there'd been a steady stream of ill-humored repartee between them. Lately, however, it'd taken a turn for the caustic.

After a final round of coffee, cheese, and vitriol, I

gladly returned to my cabin. But only to find myself confronted by a scene of far more gruesome combat....

II

The furniture had all been knocked askew and splatters of blood were everywhere. My eyes quickly gravitated to the tableau not-so-vivant near the epicenter of the mutual slaughter. There rested the half-naked bodies of two of my dear wives—Envy and Pride. The latter lay on the floor, topside up, and the former upon her in the same orientation. It took me a few moments to deduce the circumstances of their communal demise, but being an avid student of the Holmesian method, I eventually arrived at the solution.

Pride had twisted Envy's right arm behind her back while choking her with her own left one. Meanwhile, Envy had managed to reach behind and grab a clump of her sister's red bob, simultaneously sinking her teeth into the limb endeavoring to asphyxiate her. I imagine there was a good deal of flailing about at that point in the proceedings, and eventually they lost their footing. They came down on the edge of the metal bunk. Somehow they both managed to crease their skulls, and almost in the same spot. I checked them for pulses, but came up short.

I must have given forth an involuntary expostulation on seeing their mortal wounds, because soon after, Horatio entered.

"I *thought* I heard some fuss in here a while back," he said.

"Why didn't you stop them?"

"What, come between a man and his wife? ...and his

other wife? No, not me, boss. Look at that blood."

"I wonder what they were fighting about?"

"Well, the redhead came by and said you told her to wait for you in your cabin. Then a few minutes later the chubby girl came and said the same thing. I think they were fightin' over you, Captain. Musta heard about you with their greedy sister night before last. Watcha gonna do with the corpses? Bury 'em at sea?"

"I'll have to think that over. For the time being, better keep this under your hat."

"Sure.... No tellin' how sister Wrath will take it...."

When he'd gone, I knelt down and checked Envy again for a pulse. Thankfully, I felt one now—weak, but steady. And in Pride as well. I suppose it takes a lot to extinguish a Mortal Sin.

"Christ almighty!" Albertson had entered. "I always figured you fer a wife beater."

"What?" On rising, I realized I'd gotten my arms covered in blood examining the girls. "Don't be a fool—they did this to each other."

"*Sure* they did.... And you out to save American womanhood! Fat chance!"

"Just go get the first-aid kit."

I dampened a cloth and wiped their head wounds. When he returned with the kit, I dressed them as well as I could. Then we placed the girls beside each other on the bunk. Albertson left shaking his head and muttering about my unmanly behavior. He'd certainly become tiresome.

"My gods! What happened here?" It was Avarice. She'd arrived without my noticing and now seemed to be taking great amusement in the scene. "Family life. Nothing like it, is there?"

"They appear to have had a falling out."

"Well, if that's your story, I'll go along. But just out of professional curiosity, what did you use on them? Blackjack? Or the traditional cudgel?" Beyond the banter, she showed not the slightest interest in her sisters' well-being. "We've more serious matters to discuss. We'll go into town just after two. The Pelican should be crowded then."

"I'm afraid your father, or Smedley at least, beat us to it." I handed her the newspaper with the account of my arrest.

She read it carefully. "No. It says they arrested him as soon as he entered the bar. The money must still be there."

"Well, there's really no point in my taking the risk anyway. The manager there said he'd never met Smedley."

"Yes, but Smedley told them you resemble each other. So the manager will be expecting someone who looks like him. And since the authorities think they have you in custody, there will be no risk."

"*Less* risk, maybe."

"Believe me, if you don't cooperate, your risk will be all but certain." Her lips invoked the menacing curl which never failed to convince. "What exactly were you tried for?"

"The details are rather convoluted, but essentially, I hijacked a load of booze from a schooner owned by the woman who seems to be running Nassau."

"Oh, dear."

"Yes. And the sentence was abandonment at sea— without a frying pan."

"Colorful."

"I'm sure your father will come to Smedley's defense before that happens."

"Are you kidding? Nassau is the one place pirates aren't welcome. Father likely is staying well offshore."

"I see. Well, maybe Smedley will at least get the frying pan."

She smiled, then pulled my face toward hers and planted on it one of the most passionate kisses I'd ever experienced. "I'll see you at two." Her voice had never sounded so seductive.

Dumbly, I watched her leave—then turned to see Envy up on her elbows in bed. It was the awakening of her sister that prompted Avarice's osculatory performance. And it had exactly the effect she'd intended.

Envy's eyes narrowed, her forehead creased, and her lips took on the menacing curl her sister's had exhibited so recently. I wasn't certain of her train of thought—until a few moments later when she had me half-undressed and pinned to the floor. This session was every bit as energetic as our first encounter up in the ship's hold—but a good deal messier. In the excitement, her wound opened up, and then the one gracing my head did as well. If we hadn't been brought to utter exhaustion a scant hour later, we would have both been in serious danger of death by blood loss.

It was while we re-dressed each other's wounds that I noticed Pride stirring on the bed.... I fled the scene posthaste, seeking shelter with Clio up in her library.

She was cataloguing one of her new acquisitions.

"*Aethiopica*, it's called. A Greek romance by Heliodorus. This is the first French translation, the one by Jacques Amyot."

"Gripping read?"

"Well, the book has always had a special significance for me. There are parallels with my own story. You see, it tells of a baby born to the king and queen of Ethiopia. They, of course, were Africans, but the baby was born white."

"Oh.... The iceman?"

"The queen, Persinna, explained the miracle had come about because she'd gazed upon a painting of a naked, ivory-skinned Andromeda...."

"And the king bought that yarn?"

"Oh, yes. It is a romance, after all...."

"Maybe so, but I'll bet he beheaded the iceman just the same.... Wait a minute. Are you saying that your mother used the same ploy? She'd been gazing on a painting of a naked African?"

"Flipping through back issues of *National Geographic* in her gynecologist's waiting room."

"Ah. And the mad Bonnet swallowed that?"

"Well, he appreciated the literary homage. Whether he beheaded anyone, I can't say."

"Do you believe it?"

"Why not? Who wouldn't want their own origin myth? Though I might not be so sanguine had it been an article on the avifauna of New Zealand."

"Yes, a little *too* exotic.... Speaking of your father, if that was Sesbania who boarded his launch, what's likely to happen to her?"

"Well, he wouldn't marry her, if that's what you're thinking. He's a classicist. Maybe she'll be hired to work in the kitchen."

"Wouldn't be much use there."

"You know, I was just thinking of your situation. If your real wife, or supposed wife, was the one on board last night, then it was the false one who took the boat to Mayagüez...."

"Yes, that's right."

"Desecheo."

"Desecheo?"

"It's an island in the Mona Passage, between Hispaniola and Puerto Rico, not far from Mayagüez."

"Why would she go there?"

"It's a lesser pirate haven... and the rumored home of her former lover, La Baza."

"The Cyclops?"

"Yes, Caliban. She must be going back to him. Poor girl. It's up to you to save her!"

"Of course, if it's at all feasible.... But my plate's rather full just now, what with the real Sesbania's disappearance.... And Avarice's insistence I accompany her to The Merry Pelican later tonight."

"The same barroom that Smedley was arrested in? Does that seem wise?"

"Far from it. But neither does crossing your sister."

"You aren't becoming uxorious, are you?"

"Funny you should use that word. No, I'm not under her spell. Just afraid of dying."

"Well, I wish you luck. By the way, your head's bleeding again. Those sisters of mine can never stop short of drawing blood...."

She rebandaged my wound, then allowed me to nap on the cot she had set up behind the circulation desk.

Sometime after two that morning, I was woken by Avarice threatening to unman me with a letter opener.

"You know, some men's wives wake them with a kiss."

"Christ, how insipid."

I dressed and followed her to the control room. Then at the last minute, we decided to allow Melpomene to come along. She was anxious for another opportunity in the spotlight, and we figured no matter how it went down, it would prove a diversion. Not so diverting as Pride's performance in St. Pierre, perhaps. But that Sin was in no condition to reprise her brazen unraveling to the tune of *Hookshop Kate*.

As it happened, the tragedian never got the chance to take the stage. On entering the barroom, we were greeted by the lady ruler's chief henchman. The same man who'd been responsible for my arrest on my prior visit. And the destruction of Wilbur, the Navy airship my crew and I had arrived on.

"Well, well. Look who's here." I rated his tone as inauspicious.

I offered to buy him a drink and he responded by having the three of us bound and gagged. Unsociable, certainly—but at least it saved me the price of a drink.

They'd obviously been lying in wait for us. He ordered five of his men to take the two women back to the ship and see that no one got on or off. Then he and the rest shoved me along to a large house near the outskirts of town. Once inside, I was left standing under guard in an antechamber while he went off to another room. Ten minutes later, he returned and gestured to the guard to follow with me.

We entered a large dimly lit room with tall windows and a ceiling fan providing a faint breeze. From its furnishings, I took it to be an informal study. A woman was seated behind a massive desk, writing busily. She wore a linen dress, and was smoking a cigarette. It glowed unusually brightly in the darkness.

III

"Untie him and fetch the other." It was my erstwhile judge, the de facto leader of the rum-runner colony. She hadn't looked up from her desk, but I knew the voice.

Her minions untied me and removed the gag.

"Thank you," I said. "I'm glad to finally—"

"Speak again without having been spoken to, and I'll have your tongue removed."

I thought she'd chosen her words for mere rhetorical effect, but no sooner had she uttered them than the junior henchman to my right revealed a pair of rusty pliers from under his tattered shirt, and simultaneously, a toothless grin upon his misshapen face. The evocative imagery did much to clarify her intent.

Smedley entered the room at the point of a cutlass. We exchanged looks, but he stayed mum. No doubt he'd been given a similar caution by our hostess.

"Leave us," she said.

"You sure?" her chief toady asked.

She slowly lifted her eyes from the desk and directed an icy gaze upon him. He and his underlings left the room with a swiftness of movement they'd not hitherto exhibited.

"Name?" she asked me.

"Smedley." My mind had not been idle—the inevitable sentence of death making that all but impossible. "Formerly detained by the mad pirate Captain Bonnet. But now, having regained liberty through a clever ruse—"

"What nonsense!" my alter ego shouted. "He's just desperate to escape punishment."

"But not you?" she asked.

"Look, if I knew you were looking for my identical

119

twin, would I have even come ashore here?"

"Ditto," I said.

"Oh, Christ.... Ask one of his wives."

"One of his *wives?*"

"Seven altogether. *He's* this Van Slyke fellow you want. Look, as I've told you, I'm Brice Smedley. Son-in-law and secretary to Captain Bonnet. I know you're not terribly fond of pirates, but he's really in the same game you are, only with slight variations...."

"Enough! It really matters little which of you is which. You're both guilty of piracy and there's only one punishment.... But if I don't get the truth now, I'll first let Oscar loose on you both."

"Oscar?" I asked. "He wouldn't be the fellow who wields the pliers, would he?"

"He usually starts off with the pliers. Then it's... well, we haven't time to go into that. Now, one last chance: *who are you?*" Her icy gaze was now fixed on yours truly.

"All right. I'm Van Slyke."

"Good. Now we're getting someplace. Gotnik!"

At mention of his unfortunate name, the head henchman returned.

"Your Graciousness?"

"Take that one away.... Oh, and see if there are any boats heading east today."

I turned to go with him, but she stopped me.

"Not you, you fool. The pirate, Smedley."

"Now wait just a minute—" He may well have had a sound counterargument, but he wasn't given the opportunity to share it.

When the two of them had left the room, she beckoned me to a chair opposite the desk.

"Do you still claim you arrived here on a U.S. Navy airship?"

"Well…"

"Oh, quit trying to play me and answer!"

"Yes. I imagine the wreckage is still on the beach over on Andros Island."

"Nothing of use. That ass Gotnik saw to that. Might I assume you are in the same arm of the Navy that maintains seaplanes?"

"Seaplanes?"

"Are you claiming not to know what a seaplane is?"

"Oh, I know what it is. I just didn't realize you knew about them. I haven't seen any planes here at all."

"No. Nor automobiles, or trucks—nothing powered by petroleum."

"So… you're from the other side as well?"

"Arrived about three years ago."

"You work fast. I mean, to have garnered the position you have."

"Do you remember Mark Twain's book, *A Connecticut Yankee in King Arthur's Court*? It's a little like that."

"Just how, exactly?"

"Much like you, I arrived here unintentionally. Having delivered a load of liquor to Miami by seaplane, I was heading back to Nassau—the real Nassau. I hit a storm, and wound up here."

"So you shared the technology with the inhabitants?"

"Are you kidding? What sort of an ass do you take me for? One of the first things I learned was that liquor runs cheaper in this world—by thirty percent, at least. Now suppose I could master the crossing over from one world to the other."

"Ah. Buy the liquor here, fly it to the real world, sell it, bring back the profits...."

"...And live like a queen."

"What did you determine was the secret to crossing over and back?"

"Surely you jest. If you learned that, it would only necessitate my reintroducing you to Oscar."

"I see. So why are you telling me any of this?"

"Crossing over requires a speed these steam airships aren't capable of. So we've been working our seaplane pretty hard—three, four, sometimes five trips a week. Now the engines have had it. And I'm told they're beyond repair. Which leaves me in something of a predicament."

"Ah. No seaplane, no profits...."

"...no fiefdom. And I've gotten rather attached to the feudal lifestyle."

"Yes, I can see why you would. Well, I'll help in any way I can."

"I assumed you would. As soon as it's light out, I can show you the plane. In the meantime, tell me about these wives of yours. Is it true you have seven?"

"Seven wives and a misplaced fiancée—not to mention the misplaced fiancée's misplaced doppelganger."

I told her the whole sordid tale. She insisted on details, and she got them—including those of that eventful night spent with Pride and Wrath under the influence of the motivating perfume. Throughout it all, she sat there as if transfixed, interrupting only to whisper breathlessly, "Go on," whenever I paused.

My account had an effect on her similar to the one the aphrodisiac had on other women. But she came at it much more slowly. As incongruous as it may sound, she was full of inhibition, and it took some time before I was able to maneuver her over to the daybed beside the open windows.

She had to be past thirty-five, as there were the beginnings of crow's-feet forming about her eyes. And she was tall, or at least seemed that way because she was of so linear a build—her behind a modest one, and her breasts hardly apparent beyond the slight prominence of the areolas.

As it happens, I've a theory that the sensitivity of a woman's nipples is inversely proportional to the volume of her chest, and my research on her argued in favor of the hypothesis. She, on the other hand, seemed surprised at her own reaction.

"Oh, my God... oh, God...."

I'd never heard Jehovah invoked with such repetition as I did that morning. I worked down to her lap, and then had to advise her how to position herself. She was a novice, but any trace of reserve was by then long gone. Her appreciation of my efforts was gratifying, but I only wish she'd taken up paganism—at least the Greek pantheon would have provided some variation.

I finished inside her—however, she was anything but. She brought my mouth back to her for-the-nonce neglected nipples, and it was once more around the park. By sunrise, we'd made a third, fourth, and fifth circuit—I attributed my ability to stay in the game to the seafood the Frenchmen had served at dinner.

We enjoyed a leisurely breakfast out on the terrace—she almost bashful when we were alone, but forceful, bordering on dictatorial, whenever anyone else entered. During the meal, she divulged some of her own details—those of the sort I'd not discovered for myself—including her name, Gertie.

When we'd finished, she led me to a pier and the gigantic wooden hangar that housed her seaplane. I was surprised to see it was a flying boat of the Curtiss NC class. Very few of the huge craft had ever been built. I was equally surprised to find a member of my former crew present: Dombrowski, the Italian. He'd been in the hospital when we made our escape aboard *Lucy's Revenge*.

"I was beginning to think I'd never set eyes on the rest of you again. How's Cartwright?"

"Married off. As are most of the others. I'll explain later. Albertson's still aboard."

"Oh. Him I can do without. Haven't had a sound night's sleep since he bent my nose."

"He's reformed. Has a replacement for that Dorie we left behind in New York. Her twin, in fact. I take it you've been trying to fix the engines?"

"No way to do it. Two have cracked engine blocks. And every valve, rod, and piston's been worn to nubbins. I tried findin' a machine shop that could custom-make parts, but there's somethin' different in the steel they use. It can't take the heat."

"Simpler alloys, maybe."

"Yeah, somethin' like that."

"I've heard a rumor," Gertie interrupted. "There may be another seaplane to be had."

"Where?"

"Trinidad, Port of Spain. But from the little I've gathered, I don't think they know about crossing over. If that's true, they probably only have a limited amount of fuel. There's no place to acquire it on this side. I've got to stock up on every return trip. What I need is for someone to go to Trinidad and get that plane for me. I've thought of sending one of my own crews, but they'd more likely than not blow that up as well. Would you...?"

"Of course. We'll need some of your fuel, and your pilot, to fly it back."

"*I'm* the pilot. Couldn't take the risk of training anyone else. And I can't afford to leave. Your airship should be able to carry it. I doubt it's anything like the size of this."

It might have seemed an awkward time to bring up my compensation, given the affection which had passed between us a scant hour or two before—but not so awkward as leaving the matter unsettled.

"If I do, I'll want two seats on the first flight back for myself and... a companion."

"All right.... But this companion... you could choose just one of your wives?"

"My misplaced fiancée. Assuming she turns up. You wouldn't happen to know anything about a pirate ship manned by Amazons and christened *The Midnight Sun*? It's captained by a woman who calls herself Marpesia."

"Again, rumors. Is it her you suspect of having raided the S.S. *Paris*?"

"Yes. They kidnapped my fiancée. And not merely suspect—one of the other women abducted is traveling with me now and gave me the lowdown."

"Not another wife?"

"Thankfully, no. Married to the harem's steamfitter."

"The harem's steamfitter? I suppose maintaining a seraglio is no mean feat."

"Frankly, more trouble than it's worth."

"Well, I could save a berth for you here. Assuming

you get that seaplane for me... and you can forget about that misplaced fiancée of yours...."

She was interrupted by the excited approach of a one-eared ruffian. "It's bloody murder!" he cried.

"What are you talking about?" his lady asked. "Weren't you supposed to be guarding the airship?"

"Yeah, me an' four others. But they all got thoughts about the females we were guardin'. Resnick made a pass at the sultry blonde on the way there, took her behind a shed. Never saw him again. Then Jewett made a lewd suggestion to a bedraggled redhead. She skinned him and the other two alive! An' I went and hid in the galley."

"What happened to your ear?"

"Well, since I was there anyway, I ordered the French cook to make me an omelet."

"And he sliced off your ear instead?"

"No, he only did that when I told him the omelet could use some salt."

"Ah, serves you right," she said, then turned to me. "Well, have a pleasant trip."

CHAPTER 7.

THE EYES HAVE IT

Happily, the carnage had been cleaned up by the time I arrived back at *Lucy*. But I caught the crew making preparations to abandon me once again. I said nothing, expressing my disappointment with a look of reproof and a shake of the head.

Albertson shrugged. "Took another vote."

I chose not to ask the tally—the lone vote in my favor the last round was no longer aboard. Instead, I busied myself plotting a course for Port of Spain—a straight shot, due southeast. I gave Horatio the heading.

"Not going after that wife of yours?"

"Well... There's no telling where she's gone."

"Went aboard Captain Bonnet's launch, didn't she?"

"Yes, but we've no idea where he's gone. And we have a commission to attend to in Trinidad."

"Do we? What commission?"

"I'm afraid I'll need to keep that to myself for now."

"Well, suit yourself. But better OK it with the boss."

"What boss?"

"Your gal Avarice."

"Look here, who's captain of this vessel?"

"Well, you might be captain. But she put Albertson and me on the payroll—which is more than you ever done. That makes her the boss. You go check with her."

I found the greedy one soaking in the now fully functional bathhouse.

"*You know the rules!* No men outside of designated hours."

"I apologize for the intrusion, but I think we need to have a consultation. I've just learned of your attempt to subvert my authority with the crew."

"*Your authority!* Don't make me laugh. Your authority has never extended beyond your own petty mind. I wanted their loyalty and bought it on the open market. Had it ever occurred to you to *pay* them?"

"It was on my agenda."

"Yes, I'm sure it was. By the way, don't think you're getting a share of last night's take."

"Last night's? You went back?"

"Of course. One of those unfortunates dragged me off in hopes of having his way with me. Once he was dispensed with, I went back—appreciably angrier. And a little bloodier. On seeing me, the manager agreed to terms quite readily."

"I see. Well, that should content you for now. In the meantime, I've a commission to attend to."

"The only thing you need to attend to is *me!*"

"What... now? Here?"

I felt utterly exhausted—nonetheless, there *was* something compelling in her watery pose. I'd never seen her form on such complete display, nor so tastefully illuminated. Percival was that rare steamfitter with a keen aesthetic sensibility.

"Oh, get your mind out from between my legs! What is this commission you're talking about?"

"There's something I need to look into down in Port of Spain."

"Oh, Port of Spain? Why didn't you say so...."

"Not another beleaguered pelican?"

"This one's not so passive—he's hiding there incognito.... The Ugly Toucan, it's called."

"Very shrewd. All right, maybe we can kill two birds with one stone."

"Oh, *please....*"

I'd just left her when I heard the first *splat.* The ship shivered. Then came another *splat,* and another....

"What is it?" Liz had emerged from the cabin Percival had built them just off the bathhouse.

"If I had to venture a guess, I'd say my father-in-law wishes an audience."

"Bonnet?"

"Yes, the mad pirate himself."

"What luck! Now we can liberate the much-wronged Orithyia."

"Would you mind if we called her Sesbania? Sounds not so... piratical."

"What you call her isn't important—just so you're ready to fight for her return."

"If you remember, she left of her own volition. And boarded Bonnet's ship by choice."

"So? You need to prove to her how much you care...."

Splat!

"Of course. But maybe it would be better to wait for more auspicious circumstances. For the moment, evasion would seem a wiser course. Bonnet's likely to be pretty annoyed with us."

"That's all the more reason to act! If he finds out Sesbania is your... Can a man married seven times have a fiancée?" *Splat!* "Never mind. The point is, we need to save the girl!"

"Yes. I suppose you're right."

"Let me suit up and I'll meet you in the control room—oh, and rouse your wives.... They're bound to know Bonnet's weak points."

No sooner had she gone back to her cabin than Avarice emerged from the bathhouse, wrapped in a towel.

"It's Father!"

Splat!

"Yes, I recognized his calling card."

"We have to fight him off."

"Liz thought you and your sisters might know of some vulnerability...."

"Well, his principal vulnerability is that he has no crew. Urania does the navigating, and one of the Fates is usually at the helm. But no actual crew. That is, unless your former company has signed articles with him."

"If they have, *that* will be his greatest vulnerability.... Are you saying he gets by on bluff alone?"

"Not entirely. He himself is thoroughly homicidal. And Smedley's a very able swordsman...."

"He, at least, is safely locked away in Nassau.... Liz plans to board your father's ship and rescue my fiancée, Sesbania."

"Poison Ivy? Is this the real one?"

"Maybe. Our intelligence comes secondhand."

"Well, good luck to you. My sisters and I will keep anyone from boarding *Lucy*, but none of us will go back aboard Father's ship—even for a moment."

"All right. Last time, your father arrived via the crow's nest."

"Ah, excellent. I'll send Wrath and Pride up to greet him."

Down in the control room, I found the crew, their consorts, and the French cooks in conference.

"Vote's six-naught—we surrender," Horatio told me.

"Well, there are eight women up above determined to fight. Take it up with them."

A moment later, Liz and Percival appeared—she in full pirate-girl regalia.

"You must stay behind, sweetie," she told him.

"If I must...." He looked very likely to survive the humiliation.

"Who else is coming with us?" she asked.

By the time she completed her sentence, the others had vanished.

"Good, just the two of us. It will make things easier."

I thought of asking her to elaborate on her reasoning, but she'd already gone into action. She opened a window and grabbed one of the cow-gut tentacles, then slit the first couple feet in half with her dagger. The two free ends she tied to *Lucy*'s framework.

"Perfect," she pronounced. "Now we just crawl through it and—"

She was cut short by a shot of hot steam emerging from the torn tentacle.

"Won't we risk arriving parboiled?" I asked.

"Pah! What's a little heat? You go first. Go on!"

"No, I insist, ladies first."

"What *lady*?" She had her menacing manner back, and her cutlass aimed at my throat. "Get going!"

I looked back at Percival. He shrugged, then asked rhetorically, "Girl's got to go pirate every once in a while, don't she?"

Liz gave him a peck on the forehead—then me a poke with her cutlass.

One advantage of entering that animated steam bath was that it made dawdling out of the question. I scampered across as I'd never scampered before. And Antiope—as she insisted I call her during the raid—scampered just as fleetly to my aft.

"We should be inside their ship now. Go ahead and cut through—but carefully. Cut too much and...."

"And?"

"Well, we plunge to our deaths, of course."

"Ah." I cut a very modest hole and found it surprisingly easy to slip through, partly because I was by then thoroughly covered in a lubricating sweat, and partly because Antiope gave me another motivating jab with her cutlass.

We emerged in a large gallery, where the tentacles were hooked up to specialized steam pistons. Luckily, the controls must have been elsewhere, as there was no one about.

"Now it's just a matter of finding the much-wronged Orithyia...."

"Couldn't we at least agree on a less accusatory epithet? How about the fair-haired Orithyia?"

"You've *got* to be kidding! It's no wonder she keeps deserting you. Come along, weak-kneed Pluribus, we have to hurry."

The enormity of the task quickly became obvious. Bonnet's ship had literally miles of corridors, with scores of young women wandering about, many of them veiled. Each of these we had to accost to verify she was not the much-wronged Orithyia—I mean, Sesbania. And since they themselves were more often than not of a diverting and agreeable nature, it was all I could do to keep focused on our mission.

"Whatta *you* doing here?" It was Cartwright, my former chief petty officer. He'd signed on with Bonnet at the time of my third—or perhaps it was fourth—mutiny.

Antiope spun around and pinned him to the floor, her dagger at his throat.

"We're looking for a woman who boarded in Nassau yesterday," she told him.

"Only one boarded—cuz only one was allowed off: Terpsichore—needed new taps for her shoes, she said."

"And no others came aboard? This would be a newcomer."

"Take on another woman? When he's got dozens he can't get rid of? You gotta be jokin'. Let me up, will you? I ain't even armed."

Antiope did as he asked, then went off opening doors.

"By the way, who'd you wind up with?" I asked him.

"Fortitude and Charity."

"*You lucky gob.*"

"Well, truth be told, Fortitude's a little dreary—she'll bear anythin', but no grinnin' about it. And Charity... well, a little *too* charitable—if you know what I mean...."

"This door's locked," Antiope interrupted.

"Oh, no! Get away from there!" Cartwright warned her.

Never the best approach with a pirate girl. Within seconds, she had the door chopped to pieces.

Cartwright handed me a couple wads of cotton. "Stuff this in your ears, fast. Me, I'm gettin' out of here."

As he tore down the corridor, Antiope emerged with a half-dozen comely maids. They were moaning something awful.

"Shut up, you fools!" she ordered. "We're liberating you! *Whether you like it or not!*"

Her ferocity silenced them. But by then I had a good idea of who they were.

"I think maybe we should rethink the liberation plan."

"I'd rather die than have our efforts go for naught!"

"A little extreme, don't you think? Anyway, I believe these are the Limnads."

"Who are they?"

"Nymphs of... wet places."

"Lakes, marshes, and swamps," one of their number helpfully clarified.

"Yes, that's right. And they're known to give out phony calls of distress—luring men to their doom."

"That's just an ugly rumor those damn oceanids started!" another insisted.

"Oh, please take us with you! We'll behave."

"It's already decided," Antiope told them. "Fetch your things and follow us."

I've never had much luck persuading determined women—let alone determined pirate girls.

Back aboard *Lucy*, we found Bonnet and his daughters in the galley. The mad captain was bound tightly to his chair. Pride and Wrath stood over him, daggers drawn.

"All right," he said resignedly. "You can have the four Pelicans...."

"And all rights to future franchises," Avarice added.

"Yes, yes. All right. I'll sign. Just let me get back to my ship."

His bonds were cut and he put his name to the parchment placed before him, then rose from the table. When he saw me, his face transformed into the contemptuous mien his daughters exhibited with such regularity. As they say, blood tells.

"Should have killed you when I had the chance!" Then he espied the Limnads. "What have we got here...?"

"We've freed them," Antiope told him. "*And you'll never take them back!*"

"They're all yours, girlie. Make of them what you can."

We escorted him to the tentacle-passageway. There he turned to address his daughters.

"Anyone want to give their dear papa a kiss good-bye? No?" He cackled—and there was nothing the least bit fatherly about it. "Well, so long. You won the battle, *but the war ain't over yet!*"

He began making his way slowly across. Given his bulk, it was a tight squeeze.

Wrath came up and shouted into the open end of the tentacle, "Better pick up speed, *fatso*." She slit through one of the two strips securing the passageway; it dipped. One could see the bulge of Bonnet scampering more quickly now, to a chorus of satisfied cackles from his progeny.

Personally, I wasn't feeling quite so sanguine. Bonnet's regret at not having killed me sounded sincere. What's more, he seemed determined to have another go at it. And now I had another gaggle of dangerous females to come to terms with. These Limnads scared me. Women had never had much trouble luring me to my doom—and so far, I'd only dealt with amateurs.

Bonnet's ship retracted its tentacles and appeared to be leaving the field of battle. I breathed a sigh of relief—which lasted right up until Albertson's frantic call came down from where he'd been hiding in the forward look-out station.

"Birds! Millions of them!"

"Birds?"

"Seagulls... And they're coming in for attack...."

"Oh, dear," Clio said. "Father must have called them forth."

"Your father has seagulls in his employ?"

"The seagull is the sacred bird of Mormonism. If you remember, a flock saved the early settlers from a plague of locusts devouring their crop. They would have starved otherwise."

"Slipped my mind. But just what use are they in this context?"

Soon enough, we found out....

II

I don't know what those seagulls had breakfasted on, but apparently it didn't agree with them. And now they were loosing their distress on *Lucy*'s exposed vulnerabilities.

"Make way, Horatio! It doesn't matter where, just put some distance between us and this pestilent flock."

"We are makin' way, just not very fast—I think them birds have blocked out the sun. And the rudder ain't budgin'."

"You *must* find a way.... *Or else!*" Avarice shouted at no one in particular. Her tone had the familiar threatening ring to it. But for the first time, it also betrayed a measure of anxiety.

"You can't outrun Fate," Clio said prophetically. "And Father has all three working for him...."

"*Hah!*" sister Wrath rejoined. "Who needs to outrun them, when disemboweling is so much more effective...."

She cackled, but not a hearty cackle. Yes, even she was feeling uneasy—though not to the same degree as Melpomene, who rent her robe and fell to the floor, writhing in misery and wailing lamentations in Greek, Latin, and Hebrew. No doubt about it: when it came to airing anguish, she led the field.

They had good reason to worry. They'd wronged their father as few daughters would dare—first by theft, and finally through his humiliation. And yet for them, there was more to it than that. The incontinent flock was not just a foul obstacle, it was an omen. The sacred birds had to have come in the service of one vengeful god or another. All quite ridiculous, but I suppose if you're going to fish in the pool of mythology for wives, you have to expect superstition will rear its ugly head sooner or later.

"It's *your* fault!" Pride screamed at her greedy sister. *"It was all your idea!"*

"Yes," Envy agreed. "And what do I have to show for it? *Trinkets!* While you're already sitting on another hoard of gold...."

"Perhaps if we give what's left to Father, he'll not be so angry," Clio suggested.

"Over my dead body!" Avarice, sounding much like her normal self, charged up to the harem to defend her cache.

Her sisters followed—Wrath looking downright gleeful. I doubt she felt any preference for one side or the other, only for the prospect of a fight.

"We're picking up speed," Horatio announced.

This came as no surprise. *Lucy* produced steam by means of human exertion, and though bickering Sins could only loosely be called human, the vigor they put into the bickering more than made up for any shortfall.

"If they keep at it long enough, we might get away. What about the rudder?"

"Still no use."

We were heading east. Not the direction of Port of Spain, but at least we were outrunning Bonnet's ship. And the seagulls seemed finally out of ammunition.

When two hours later the ship slowed, I sent Reynard upstairs with a plate of just three éclairs. Sins, of course, don't know the meaning of the word share. By the time the pastry chef limped back down, we were once more making speed.

When a thick bank of dark clouds rolled in below us, I descended into the cloudburst, hoping a hard rain might free our rudder. But just as I did so, the wind picked up. Rather than free the rudder, the squall rendered the elevators inoperable. Now we could neither steer nor rise above the storm.

We drifted downward. I tried releasing ballast, but it had all been expended earlier during our escape from Bonnet. I could see only water below us.

"Tell me, Horatio, do steam airships float?"

"You kidding? Sink like a stone. That's why they usually come with a few boats."

"When you say usually, I assume you're drawing a distinction in regard to *Lucy*. We don't have any sort of boats, do we?"

"No.... Maybe we could make a raft?"

"Good idea. Any wood aboard?"

"No, no wood. How about we lash together those wives of yours?"

"Good luck trying."

"Land ho!" Albertson shouted—about three seconds after the crash.

"What serendipity. An island."

"Yes, but *which* island?" Horatio asked.

"What's it matter, just so it floats?"

About half an hour later, the storm passed as quickly as it had appeared. We went out to inspect the ship. The heavy downpour had cleared the rudder. And the elevators were once again operable. But all the propellers on the starboard side had been bent in the crash.

"Can we fix them?" I asked.

"Well, easier to buy new ones. But this island don't look big enough to harbor airships. We'll have to take them off and coax them back into shape."

"Coax them?"

"Sure. *Lucy*'s parts is delicate. Could take a day or two."

"Well, you can get Albertson and Percival to help with the coaxing. In the meantime, I'll reconnoiter."

"How about *I* reconnoiter and *you* coax?"

"You're on more intimate terms with *Lucy*."

"That's true. All right, but don't be gone too long or we might take another vote."

Lucy had come down in a small valley between two ridges. I climbed to the top of the taller ridge and discovered the island didn't extend more than a mile in any direction. We'd been lucky. With my binoculars, I scanned for signs of habitation. I saw only one. Off to the west, further along the same ridge, someone had constructed a primitive tower.

I headed in that direction and soon came upon a well-trodden path. I followed that for a few hundred yards, until it ended in a clearing on the south side of the ridge. Here there were various hints of recent tenancy—empty wine bottles, the remains of a fire, and, hanging from a line strung between two trees, an assortment of ladies' undergarments. They were damp, but not so wet they'd been there during the storm. Someone had just put up her washing. And based on the dimensions of her negligee, I judged she was someone worth meeting.

The tower was just above me now, and I climbed up to see if I could determine where this female resided. I saw no sign of any structure whatsoever. A puzzle, certainly. A woman living so primitively she has no shelter— but a clothesline-full of silk lingerie. One could only imagine her idea of hospitality.

I searched the brush in every direction from the clearing, but found no other paths. It was evening by then, and I'd need to leave soon in order to reach the ship before dark. I'd just taken one last turn about the clearing, when suddenly a rock up ahead seemed to move. I dropped to the ground, and then watched as a woman ascended from the earth wearing nothing but a man's shirt.

There were two features to this female which struck me as familiar. First, I identified the shirt as my own by a tear on the right sleeve. I'd been wearing it during my last escape from Barataria. Second, I recognized the five-spotted mole which graced the girl's right bum. It was one or the other Sesbania.

After fumbling the placement of their respective moles repeatedly, I'd inscribed the fingers of my left hand with the letters R-E-A-L, and my right with F-A-U-X. So, I reasoned, this was the stand-in.

She was pinning a blouse to the clothesline. Not wanting to startle her, I called to her as gently as possible. "Psst. It's me, Pluribus."

Rather than being alarmed, she presented me with the most thoroughly joyous countenance either Sesbania had ever evinced. Within a twinkling, she'd flown over and had her arms about my neck.

"You came for me! I dreamed you would.... But how did you know where I was?"

It appeared I had a loving reunion in store—just so long as I didn't muck it up. Luckily, my conversation with Clio provided me the answer.

"Well, naturally I deduced you were heading back here, to Desecheo. Why else go to Mayagüez?"

"Yes, I see. But what made you decide to come?"

I was on trickier ground here. "Feelings I can't adequately express...."

"Oh, me either!"

That was all well and good, but my thoughts now gravitated to her erstwhile consort, the Cyclops Clio tellingly referred to as Caliban. "I suppose that La Baza fellow is off rum-running somewhere."

"Yes... but he and his men are due back tonight. We'll need to leave the island at once."

"Ah. There's a slight hitch there. Our ship required some repairs and I doubt if they're completed."

"Oh. Well, let me gather my things, then we can hide in the brush until it's ready."

She made for the rock-door, but just as she got to it, it popped open and up jumped an orange-haired giant.

"*Where's my dinner?*" he bellowed.

He was tall, half a foot taller than me, and had the sort of disagreeable aspect one expects a giant to exhibit. He was, however, not strictly speaking a Cyclops—a piratical patch covered his right eye. (In case you haven't noticed, I plan on getting my money's worth out of that adjective.)

The wise course would have been for her to descend with him, and then sneak out later while he slept. Had she, she could have expected to find me waiting—if at all humanly possible. I'm sure that's the course the real Sesbania would have chosen. But faux Sesbania was not so calculating.

"Never again will I make a meal for you! Or share your bed! My one true love has come to claim me! And, if need be, destroy you!"

She'd gotten a little ahead of herself there. We might have stood a reasonable chance running off into the brush. But my giant-slaying skills were rudimentary, at best. She'd indicated my position by a tilt of her head, and the brute was now facing me. He straightened himself and appeared to grow another six inches.

I'd been using my cutlass as a machete, but dropped it when faux Sesbania rushed me. Now I leaned over to pick it up. In a flash, he leapt at me and brought a knee under my chin. I eventually landed against a tree, whereupon an avalanche of yellow-green fruit came down on top of me.

The beast swung his own cutlass at me, but I rolled out of the way and was soon on my feet. Weaponless, I picked up a dead branch from the ground. It was a mere wisp from some thorny shrub, but just long enough to reach his face. We parried for some time. I was the smaller, and less well armed—but also without an angry female affixed to my back biting off an ear.

Several of his strokes had drawn blood, while I'd not managed to so much as scratch him. Then, by mere chance, I happened to poke him in his one good eye. Blinded, he wheeled about, screaming in misery. Faux Sesbania dropped from his back and ran to me.

"We should get out of here," she said.

"I couldn't agree more."

"Wait! Help me carry some of these mangoes. They're nearly ripe, and I do so love them."

Having foolishly acquiesced to her request, I'm able to share yet another bit of botanical trivia with you: the skin of the mango contains the very same allergen as poison ivy.

III

With the last glimmer of sunlight, we reached *Lucy*, already six feet off the ground. I drew two conclusions from this. First, the repairs were simpler than Horatio had expected; and second, they'd taken another vote.

We clambered up one of the dangling lines and arrived in the control room to find Avarice once more issuing edicts.

"You seem to have a knack for last-minute entrances," she said. "Oh, and you found Poison Ivy! How sweet."

"This isn't Poison... I mean, Sesbania. This is... By the way, what *is* your name?"

"Clematis."

"Clematis?"

"Yes, you know, the vine. Virgin's Bower."

"*How trite!*" the greedy one opined. "Well, I'll leave you to your deflowering. I never finished my bath this morning."

She glided up the ladder.

"Don't worry about her," I told my secondary climber. "She only thinks she's in charge. You might be able to find something to wear in the cabin. If not, we can have you fitted for a robe."

"Oh, I left a few things here. Just in case...."

Why did I have the feeling I'd once more been tested?

Horatio was at the helm throughout this—saying nothing, but expressing his amusement just the same.

"You sure who she is this time?" he asked.

"Yes. I've got the bums straight now." I showed him the back of my hands.

"Ah, good thinking."

"So you didn't have much trouble straightening the propellers?"

"No—not once we locked up those new girls in the bathhouse."

"The Limnads?"

"Yes. Started singing songs to us. Makin' promises, if you know what I mean."

"I can guess."

"You plannin' on marryin' them too?"

"No, I don't need any help in hurrying my doom."

"No, don't suppose you do. Well, soon as we locked them up, your greedy wife showed up with her horse-whip. Accused us of dawdling. Bein' on her payroll's like workin' the old plantation. Job got done in no time."

"If it's any consolation, she doesn't treat spouses much better."

"Maybe. But least you get the perks."

"I don't notice any loose buttons on you...."

He laughed.

Both Clio and Melpomene joined us for dinner in the mess that evening, where faux Sesbania—i.e., Clematis—had promised to regale the company with her woeful tale. The tragedian was seeking fresh calamities, and the librarian anything bearing classical allusion.

Clematis recounted how she had wandered into La Baza's clutches in much the way Clio had conjectured. At first, she found him a romantic figure—a rich adventurer who seemed genuinely interested in a humble girl from Ohio. He swept her off her feet, and she came willingly to his island redoubt.

"You must have been pretty disappointed when he brought you to a dark cave on a barren island," I said.

"Oh, the hideout is actually quite plush, and airy. You descend through that entrance into a huge mansion built into the cliff-side. There are terraces and plate-glass windows in every room. The view is exquisite. But it wasn't long before his darker side appeared. He acts the petulant child when he doesn't get his way, lashing out in all directions. And if something goes wrong, he blames everyone but himself. Worst of all, he has the most awful taste—downright garish. I mean, who wants to sit on a gold-plated toilet?"

"Ooh, I would," Mattie confessed. "Just once. Do tell us more, Clematis."

"Call me Clem—everyone does. The first time I left him, it was in one of his own ships. Lafitte captured us and took me hostage. Well, you know what happened then. Your friend Aggie played her little trick."

"Well, you're safe here now," I said.

"Yes. Thanks to you. You should have seen how he vanquished the Cyclops," she told the others.

"How?" Clio asked. "Did you blind his lone eye with a tree you whittled to a sharp point, and hardened in a fire?"

"Ah, not exactly. But I did poke him with the spiny

branch of a shrub. Seemed to do the trick."

"Of course, he's not *really* a Cyclops," Clem told us. "Not even figuratively."

"What about the eye-patch?"

"Conjunctivitis. He can't get rid of it."

"Oh, then he shouldn't wear a patch over it. It needs air," Clio said.

"That's what I told him. But he's too vain to allow people to see the pinkeye."

"So if he would have just removed the patch, he could have come after us?"

"Yes, but he'd never do that. Especially not in front of company."

Later, in the privacy of my cabin, Clem regaled me alone with another tail. She was certainly a girl who knew how to express gratitude. But no sooner had things come to a head than she broke into tears. She was torn, she said, between joy at my having come to rescue her and shame at having imposed herself between me and Sesbania. I tried to make her feel better by itemizing her rival's more unflattering characteristics, of which I knew quite a number. Then she sobbed over how horridly everyone treated me.

"And you a poor orphan!"

On this point, at least, I was able to ease her mind. The truth is, my mother had not died soon after my birth. She'd run off with an organ salesman named Lester. My confession brought a smile to her lips—curiously, it always has that effect—but then she welled up anew.

"It's worse, really, isn't it? I mean, to have your mother abandon you while still a baby...."

Desperate times call for desperate measures. She'd had just one dose of the provocative perfume and was still good for at least one more go. I took the vial from the hiding place in my shoe. On seeing it, her eyes widened....

Well, suffice it to say, there was no time for tears after that.

Chapter 8.

A Pelican Incognito

We woke in each other's arms—but not until late the next afternoon. Clem professed to have only a vague memory of all that went on. Given that most of the program had originated in her imagination, I found that not very plausible. But just in case, I jotted down some quick notes in the ship's log for future reference, diagrams included.

It was she who brought up Sesbania, rather obliquely at first. She asked what my plans were for the future. I found myself baring my soul—and what a queer feeling *that* gave me. After a lifetime of prevarication and carefully layered deception, I was telling this girl I hardly knew my innermost thoughts. Sesbania and I had never confided our innermost thoughts. I knew her feelings toward facial hair, croissants, and railroad securities, but not her innermost thoughts.

From there, it was a small step to broaching the subject of our origins.

"I imagine you must have surmised that Sesbania, Aggie, and I all come from a different place."

"Yes, of course. Albertson tried to explain it to me once. But it left me more confused than before."

"Most conversations with Albertson end like that."

"It's not Canada, is it?"

"Ah, no, not Canada. Try imagining that you've entered a world depicted in a book. And suddenly, those people you thought of as characters are people just like you."

"Oh, I've often done that. What child hasn't? *Little Women* was my favorite.... What book is it you've come from?"

She had it backwards, obviously. But since setting her straight might prompt a metaphysical fit, I left well enough alone.

"Oh, an obscure book by a minor writer. Not something you'd ever have come across."

"How can you know if you don't tell me?"

"It's called *Capt. Billy's Whiz Bang*."

"A children's book!"

"Adolescent, certainly.... Anyway, we'll need to all get back to that world eventually."

"Why?"

"Why? Well, the... ah, the imperative of narrative integrity...."

"What in the world does that mean?"

"It's just the way things must be. I'm on a mission now to find a seaplane."

"What's a seaplane?"

"A sort of airship which makes use of differences in air flows and attendant pressures to stay aloft."

"Oh. What does that mean?"

"Not sure exactly, just quoting a textbook. Anyway, it has wings to fly with and can land in the sea."

"So can a cormorant."

"Yes, but a cormorant doesn't take passengers."

"That's true. But why do you want this seaplane?"

"I arrived here by accident, and certainly can't count on another to get me back. Apparently, there is a way to pass between the two worlds at will. But it requires more speed than a steam airship is capable of."

"And this seaplane can reach that speed?"

"Yes. If I can get ahold of it. It was last rumored to be in Port of Spain."

"So once you acquire this seaplane, you'll scoop up Sesbania and depart for the book with her…. And I'll be left behind…."

"It would seem to be in the cards."

"Is it what she wants? I heard that she came on board after I left."

"Well, she left before I realized she wasn't you, so I didn't have a chance to ask."

"But if she went off without telling you, doesn't that mean she doesn't care?"

"It's hard to say with her."

"It doesn't seem fair, really…. Say, I know! There's nothing holding me here. *I* could go back with you and play *her* part."

"That might not be so easy. There's a history involved."

"I'm a quick learner. Just let me read through the book a few times."

After what had gone on the night before, I can say quite candidly there wasn't much that *Capt. Billy's Whiz Bang* could teach this girl. But her proposal did set me to thinking.

I cared deeply for Sesbania, of course—even minus her currency-laden chemise. She possessed many of the qualities a man holds dear. And while it's true these were largely offset by a nearly equal number of qualities that same man would come to fear, there was one factor that sent the scales firmly in her favor: the countess.

I'm referring to the guardian I mentioned earlier. She was a woman with a past—and I mean that in every sense of the word. She'd been a jewel thief, an aristocrat, an influence peddler, and had had more lovers than Casanova—even, perhaps, than the proverbial iceman himself. Her powers of persuasion were notorious on both sides of the Atlantic. She could charm the skin off a snake—then turn around and sell it back to him for exactly what the market would bear.

This unique talent for speedy valuation was by no means incidental to her achievements, and may account for why she rated me so poorly. She and Sesbania fell out over her ward's decision to accompany me to Europe. Though from the very start, it was obvious that the breach was a temporary one. Sesbania couldn't go a day without relating some anecdote about her adored mentor. And inside a week, they had resumed correspondence.

The countess lived comfortably, but not lavishly— just a small staff in a nice-sized Washington townhouse. There was little doubt, however, that she had large sums socked away. And as she had no other heir, there was also little doubt that Sesbania would be inheriting her fortune. Just how vast it was, I couldn't be sure. But there were real-estate holdings, and business interests, and, I felt certain, a plethora of bank accounts on both continents. Twenty years after her death, her heir would receive a knock at the door and the news that yet another safe-deposit box had been found with a small hoard of bullion.

There was only one thing that would cause an irreparable breach and that would be our marriage. Which accounts, at least partly, for our mutual reluctance to tie the knot. Every once in a while, Sesbania would propose that we go through with it—but only to test me. If I voiced agreement, she'd quickly change her mind. We knew each other's characters too well to get anywhere with that tack.

If I wanted to get my hands on a share of the countess's fortune, I'd need to maintain Sesbania's affection and keep her from marrying anyone *else* before the old lady died. Not an easy task, certainly, but neither a wholly unpleasant one.

Sadly, the countess was not an old lady. In her late forties, I should think. And a well-preserved specimen at that. She might live into her eighties. And maintaining Sesbania's goodwill for forty years would be a pretty tall order. Just maintaining it over dinner often taxed my powers.

What if, however, I showed up with another Sesbania? One so enamored of me, she'd have no problem with the waiting. There'd be difficulties, naturally. Sesbania had known the countess since she was a child. But with some studying, Clem could pick up quite a bit of that. And for what she couldn't, there was always the old amnesia ploy. That left the telltale mole....

While those thoughts were drifting through my mind, Sesbania—I mean Clematis, of course—fell asleep in my arms. She was looking particularly beatific in the light of early evening, and that left me feeling unusually serene. But only up until someone once more violently kicked in the cabin door....

II

I didn't recognize the fellow staring down at me, but his choice of entrance struck me as decidedly piratical. Though even had he knocked, the flashy attire and plentiful jewelry would have narrowed the possibilities considerably.

"Don't tell me—Captain Lafitte?"

"Yes, Jean Lafitte, at your service." Unlike his brother, he spoke English with only the trace of an accent. Later I learned he claimed to have attended Princeton.

"Very accommodating. Then perhaps you wouldn't mind leaving as you entered?"

"Don't be impudent! It's just an expression." He drew his cutlass and placed its point against my throat. "I have come to seek my revenge! You have wronged me, and more than once! Now you must pay!"

"Well, I don't mean to split hairs, but our little tit-for-tat began with your henchman, Geoff l'Indigné, strapping me to that diabolical contraption of yours."

"He's a pirate! And *very* indignant! What did you expect, arriving without an invitation? And with that damned Jack Tigue!"

"Look, I don't think I should be dragged into your disagreement with Jack."

"Forget Jack! What about this girl you stole?"

"What right do *you* have to her, except right of conquest? And please quit yelling, or you're liable to wake her."

"Well, if you want her, maybe we can make a deal—but then there's the ruin of my auction house."

"Not my doing. The Mortal Sins got a little carried away."

"Mortal Sins? Not Bonnet's daughters?"

"The very same. It was they who destroyed your auction house."

"And filleted my men?"

"One of your men. The others were merely slaughtered. That was Wrath's doing."

"One girl did that?"

"Well, she *is* the personification of wrath. Plus, it was her time of the month."

"Ah. And do you have the complete set? All seven?"

"Just five. But do you mind if we have this conversation someplace else? Maybe you'd like some coffee and pastries?"

He agreed. However, I'd inadvertently introduced another of his grievances: his two French chefs. We found them under guard in the galley.

"Let's get one thing straight," I said. "Your cooks came here of their own free will. I certainly didn't coerce them."

"It was all Reynard's idea!" Emile, the saucier, told his erstwhile employer. He spoke in French, of course, but I believe that's what he said.

"You little rat!" the pâtissier retorted while grabbing a cleaver.

Lafitte's men held them apart.

"I'd gladly go back in a minute. This kitchen is impossible! *There isn't even a couscoussier!*"

This lack had been a bone of contention with Emile since his arrival. He was half-Algerian, his mother a Berber, and he considered the device essential. What function a couscoussier performed had never been explained.

While Lafitte and I took our coffee and croissants into the adjacent mess, the two cooks continued hurling invectives at one another. Most of it was indecipherable to me, but I did catch one interesting tidbit. The salmagundi Emile had prepared their first evening aboard had included the parrot. Frankly, knowing it at the time would have only increased my enjoyment of the meal.

Lafitte and I swiftly dispensed with our first order of

business. He was partial to Emile's béchamel, while I found cream sauces sat heavily with me. It's true my wives favored them, but the combination of rich sauces and buttery pastries was beginning to take a toll on their waistlines. I'm not the sort to embarrass a lady by bringing the matter up—especially when that lady is a Mortal Sin. Nonetheless, I think it's fair to say, one French cook per household is plenty. So we split the chefs.

That brought us back to Clem.

"Just how much did you expect her to fetch at auction?"

"I didn't expect her to go to auction. I expected La Baza to pay her ransom. They always do."

"So the auction is just a threat?"

"Let's say an inducement. Every few months I auction a girl just so they know I mean business. But it's only a performance. I've got to have a couple of my men do the bidding. Pirates prefer to rent rather than own."

"Don't want to be stuck with last year's model?"

"Yes, must be *au courant*—the little prima donnas."

"So La Baza wouldn't pay? What were you asking?"

"Just $5,000! He probably has it lying about."

"The bastard. And the girl knew that?"

"Sure, that's why she went along with Aggie's plan. By the way, what happened to her?"

"Aggie? Went off with Jack."

"Ah. Well, she'll get what she's looking for with him."

"Get what she's looking for?"

"Sure. Never seen a woman so obviously in heat."

"In heat? Aggie?"

"Sure. You didn't bed her?"

"Well, I'm not the sort to kiss and tell.... Anyway, would you be willing to take my note in exchange for the girl? Say, for $2,000."

"Three—plus five percent per annum, compounded monthly."

"I happen to know quarterly is the norm, but all right."

"That brings us to these Sins of yours."

"Wives, actually."

"Ah. That complicates things."

"Not for me, it doesn't."

"Which have you got?"

"Wrath, Envy, Pride, Avarice, and Sloth."

"Where are they?"

"First, I'd like to know what your intentions are."

"Harness their power, of course!"

"Well, good luck with that. At this time of day, should all be in the bathhouse. But I warn you, they'll put up a fight. How many men have you got?"

"Plenty—don't worry about that."

I gave him directions and he and a couple dozen of his cutthroats started up the ladder.

There was a good deal of commotion upstairs, made all the more unpleasant by Melpomene starting up with the calliope once more—I wished then I'd thought of adding her into the bargain.

The wounded began arriving not ten minutes later. First one at a time, then two or three together. But ultimately victorious, Lafitte descended with his string of females. On seeing that first shapely pair of ankles atop the ladder, I thought my contentious wives had finally met their match. However, as they emerged—their heads covered and wrists bound—I counted five more pairs of shapely ankles, or six altogether. And not one among the captives kicking, shouting, or napping. It didn't take me long to deduce that these docile ankles belonged not to my Mortal Sins, but rather to their half-sisters, the Limnads.

"Why didn't you mention you had Lust as well? Hoped I'd leave her behind?"

"Well, seemed worth a try."

The water nymphs, happy to be liberated, had gamely taken on their sisters' identities—though not their disagreeable personalities.

After a hearty round of celebratory cackles, Lafitte returned to his ship with his train of wounded pirates, pseudo-Sins, and one very uppity saucier. It wasn't clear what danger the nymphs held for a crew disinclined toward women. Seeing how Aggie had gotten nowhere with Lafitte, I assumed he, at least, would be immune. But apparently not completely. As they sailed off to the north, their ship began to zigzag erratically....

Liz had followed the lake sprites down and watched their departure with me.

"Was it you who told Lafitte they were their sisters?" I asked her.

"It was my idea, but they were all for it. To be honest, I was regretting having brought them aboard. They were distracting Percival...."

"Well, I suppose that is their mandate."

As usual, my crew only showed up after all danger had passed.

"Where were you hiding this time?"

"Hiding? Weren't hiding," Horatio insisted. "Helping Clio in the library."

"Uh-huh. Well, since you had your nap, you can get

us back on course. We should make Port of Spain by morning."

"Aye, aye." He made his silly excuse for a salute, then called after me. "Oh, I ran into your greedy wife on the way down. Says you better come and see her."

"It can wait 'til morning."

"*It* might—but *she* won't. Said she better not have to come and get you...."

A captain never wants to appear uxorious before a member of his crew—but then, neither does he wish to be disemboweled. I made my way up to my harem with even greater trepidation than usual. Who would have thought a man's harem could be a source of such dread? Not even the irony of the sentiment could cheer me.

I found her as always—on her couch, surrounded by a thick cloud of malodorous tobacco. But this time, there was nothing the least bit fetching in her pose.

"What sort of deal did you make with Lafitte?"

"Deal? He surprised me in bed."

"He said you had given us to him with your blessing."

"Oh, what calumny! You can't believe anything a man like that says."

She stared at me while taking a long drag on her hookah. "Well, you certainly didn't put up much of a fight."

"How could I? Weaponless—and abandoned by my crew. Or *your* crew, I should say."

"*Quit carping!* A wife has a right to expect her husband to make some effort."

"Is this the same wife who's tried to desert me three times in the last week?"

"I only wanted to cure you of this habit of dawdling.

And, I might note, in every case you've returned with some other female in tow."

"Not in Nassau."

"I wouldn't bring up Nassau if I were you. Perhaps you weren't aware of the marks on your neck."

"Marks on my neck?"

"Whoever you spent the night with had a taste for flesh."

Whenever a Sin seems to be exhibiting a human emotion outside her natural province—like Avarice jealousy—the wise man plays his cards close to the chest.

"I spent that night trying to avoid a sentence of certain death! This dates from earlier in the evening. If you remember, it was you yourself who woke Envy. And then egged her on with that kiss."

"Looked very fresh to me. Besides, I know my sister's bite mark. I bear the scar from one." She showed me her arm in case I had doubts. "Bitch always has to have the last chocolate…. But we'll set your philandering aside for the present. When do we reach Port of Spain?"

"Tomorrow morning—barring any further interruptions."

"Then you have time to make amends…."

As I mentioned earlier, she wasn't looking her comely best. She'd been given such a mouse her left eye was swollen shut, while a clot of dried blood on her right temple had welded itself to a shock of hair. Bruises accented one cheek and all four limbs. And for the time being, she needed to do her sneering through a very fat lip.

Which of the wounds could be attributed to the skirmish with Lafitte's pirates and which dated from the battle she and her sisters had the day before over the three éclairs, I couldn't say with certainty. The only thing

I *was* certain of was that this Sin was not in a mood to abide disobedience. I dutifully followed her into her chamber.

I zeroed in on the one bit of her anatomy which had remained unscathed, and for the better part of an hour things progressed about as they had our previous session together. It was then I discovered that bit of herbal lore I mentioned earlier, regarding the toxic properties of the mango.

"What is it? Oh, Christ! You're breaking out in red splotches...."

I tried explaining what'd caused the rash, but she seemed dubious.

"You better hope it's not infectious.... Go! Go on back to what's-her-name, your vine!"

Instead I went to the bathhouse for a cold soak. It was outside the designated hours for men, but with the Limnads having vacated, I thought I'd be safe. And I was—until Pride arrived. She still had a bone to pick over my liaison with Envy on the floor of my cabin. How much she'd witnessed was unknowable. But she now worked me even harder. What's more, she quickly discovered that having me attend to her nether regions while submerged increased her elation a hundredfold. I suppose the threat of drowning did cause me to focus my efforts.

She began singing bawdy tunes. Whenever I hit the mark with the proper rapidity, she'd quickly rise up the scale. Once she reached the high note, I was usually able to sneak in a quick breath of air. But very quick—in no time she'd push my head back down. The final coupling occurred underwater. It was my first such effort—surprising for a Navy officer, I know. But given my methodology, even if the girl wasn't a Mortal Sin, the risk of drowning was all too real.

Her vanity for the moment sated, Pride went off to the hot bath contented, and I to my cabin exhausted. I crawled in next to Clem, still fast asleep. I've met some sound sleepers in my time, but that girl really was in a class by herself. This marked the second pirate raid she'd slept through that week.

III

When Horatio woke me an hour later, I felt hardly rested at all. But I steeled myself for the work ahead. Now that we were in Port of Spain, I needed to find that seaplane as quickly as possible—and then somehow get it back to Nassau.

As Clem was the only one on board I'd been willing to trust with my mission, I brought her along to help canvass the docks. I assumed the plane would be hidden from view in some sort of hangar. But if it was ever made use of, people were bound to have seen it.

Unfortunately, no one we met. Or, at least, no one inclined to talk about it. After a fruitless morning, and a bountiful lunch, we rented bicycles and ventured up the coast road. Trinidad was far larger than I'd realized, too large for us to circumnavigate. But we could get the search started.

We'd gone ten or twelve miles and seen nothing. Now in need of a rest, we stopped to lie down along the shaded shore of a cove. I'd just closed my eyes when Clem said something about the water.

"Look how it shimmers there. It's all the colors of the rainbow."

"Oil, probably," I said absentmindedly. "Floats on the surface and refracts the light."

Slowly it hit me. I hopped up and walked over to where ripples lapped lazily against the shore. Kneeling down, I cupped some of the shimmering water. It smelled of gasoline.

"The seaplane. It's been here."

We searched about, but there seemed to be no houses or other signs of habitation. Then an old man wearing a wide hat approached, leading a burro wearing the same style of hat and pulling a cartload of fruit.

"I don't suppose you've seen a sort of airship setting down here? On the small side, with wings. And pontoons, so it can float on the water."

He looked at me warily. "No, too old. Lots I don't see. Letitia mighta seen it."

"Where can we find her?"

He tugged the burro's lead and its head bobbed. "She don't talk much."

Not much, perhaps. But when Clem produced a British crown, the coin induced a bray which Letitia's attendant interpreted for us.

"Gone."

"Gone where?"

He turned and looked at the burro.

"Letitia's keepin' mum."

A second silver crown brought another bray.

"Letitia says, up the Orinoco."

"The Orinoco? That's a large river. Can she be any more precise?"

For a third silver crown, Letitia let loose a third bray.

"No, she says."

He went on his way and we started back to Port of Spain.

"Where exactly is the Orinoco?" Clem asked.

"Venezuela. The mouth is somewhere just to our south. But it must be five hundred miles long—maybe a thousand. And I'm not sure I trust that burro."

"She looked honest enough."

We reached *Lucy* just as the sun was setting. Then after a light supper, we went off to bed. Avarice woke me sometime after midnight.

"We have an appointment in town, remember?"

"Oh. The Sultry Ibis, wasn't it?"

"Not bad. The Ugly Toucan, run by the woman who had the Pelican franchise at Fort-de-France. She decided she'd had enough of sharing profits with Father and went off on her own. The gink running The Merry Pelican in Nassau told me she was hiding down here."

"But why would she now share her profits with you?"

"Oh, Father had a team of lawyers write up the franchise agreement. If she sells a bucket of swill in Timbuktu, he's owed a share."

"He really *is* a pirate, isn't he? All right, we'll hit your barroom tonight. But first thing tomorrow, I've something to attend to up the Orinoco."

"Up whose Orinoco?"

"Whose? It's a river. Venezuela's, I guess."

"Ah. I thought it might be a euphemism. What's there?"

"Well, something I need to find. But there must be some lively ports along its banks. Maybe you can sign on another franchisee."

"Hmm. All right, why not?"

A little while later, we left *Lucy*, with Clem, as usual, sound asleep. Other airships came and went in a steady stream, so there was nothing particularly noteworthy about seeing one mooring as we passed. It was, however, an unusually large ship. And, though it was difficult to tell in the dark, it looked to be painted black. I stopped in my tracks.

"I think that might be *The Midnight Sun*."

"So?"

"So, Sesbania had been aboard her. Could be again."

"Isn't one creeping vine enough for you?"

"Climbing vine, if it's all the same to you."

"And isn't she the one who abandoned you in Nassau?"

"Well, yes—but it might have been on a whim. She can be moody."

"Not half so moody as I can be. And when I act, there'll be nothing whimsical about it. Tomorrow you can make your herbal inquiries. Tonight we have our work cut out for us."

"Another Viking?"

"Oh, no. Myra's a tiny little thing. However, she and Smedley used to be an item. One of the reasons she went off was his marriage to Euphrosyne. Quite a betrayal, as she saw it."

"Not out for blood, I hope?"

"Who knows? But just to be safe, let's tell her the insipid Graces all died from some horrible disease—I've always wished they would."

The name of the barroom was once more explained by the signage—this time, recycled signage. Someone had attempted to turn what had been a pelican into a toucan.

But it was, indeed, one *very* ugly toucan. Furthermore, the interior bore no resemblance whatsoever to the other avian taverns. Here all the men were well-behaved, and their women fully clothed. There wasn't a single pirate in sight. Nor a nipple.

Much to my surprise, Myra turned out to be the spitting image of Aggie. A cleaned-up Aggie, I should add, and one displaying far more taste in her attire. Believing me to be Smedley, she looked upon me as you might expect, displaying both hurt and anger—her moist eyes betraying the hurt, and her set mouth conveying the anger. Likewise the sharp slap across my face. So sharp, the band stopped playing, and every eye in the place turned to see the show.

Embarrassed, she made an apology to her patrons, then led us into a back room. There I muttered my own abject apology. But I left it to Avarice to inform her of my wife's demise. In her telling, the deaths of the Graces were not pleasant ones. They'd fallen into the grip of a grisly affliction, one that combined the ghastliest features of dysentery, leprosy, and the Black Death.

This news seemed to brighten Myra's mood some, and I have every confidence I'd have been able to win back her affection—if only my greedy wife hadn't too soon introduced the topic always uppermost in her mind.

"I should have known! You only came for the money. You're nothing but a filthy pirate!"

"Privateer," I corrected. But she seemed not to appreciate the distinction.

She pressed a button beneath the table and a moment later three men who were either longshoremen or heavyweight boxers entered the room.

"*You'll not get out of paying that easily!*" Avarice told her. "You have a contract!"

She was sounding darkly determined, as only a Mortal Sin can. But once the pounding started, she quite quickly ceded both the field and me to my tormenters.

These fellows were also determined—each one landing several solid blows. But it was all done reasonably fairly—one at a time, and none of this holding the other fellow's arms while your associate slugs him. Not that that bettered my odds much. I still woke battered beyond feeling and lying in a cesspool.

The sun hadn't risen, and the sky was the deep blue of twilight. Remembering Avarice's admonition about dawdling, I made my way to the ship as quickly as possible. The lines had already been released and I needed to leap into the air to get hold of one. I looked up and saw a familiar figure climbing up just ahead of me. I followed her aboard, and looked her in the eye.

"It's me, Clem," she assured me.

I smiled, but it wasn't until I got her in the cabin and lifted her skirt that I felt sure. In the meantime, I gave Horatio a course for the mouth of the Orinoco. Then watched as Avarice, looking even more dissatisfied than normal, glided up the ladder. No doubt she blamed me for the fiasco at The Ugly Toucan.

On giving me a sniff, Clem insisted I go take a shower. When I returned, she was sound asleep. I crawled in beside her and followed suit. Around noon, when Horatio woke me with the news that we'd arrived at our destination, I found her already up and dressed. She sat on the bed and told me she needed to make a confession.

"I was worried last night and went out after you."

"Well, it's just as well you didn't find me. Things didn't go as planned."

"Yes, I can see that. You know, I'm not sure you're cut out for this work."

"No need to convince me."

"Anyway, I was out looking for the bar you went off to and came across something shocking."

"What?"

"Me! ...Well, your Sesbania."

"Really? Why didn't you say so earlier?"

She shrugged.

"What happened?"

"Well, we talked. I told her how you had arranged to go back as soon as you found this seaplane thing. And I asked, point blank, if she was going to accompany you. 'No,' she said. 'I doubt I'll ever set eyes on him again.' Then, before I could even ask, she gave me her blessing to go in her place. Even told me a secret about her guardian that would convince her that I was Sesbania."

"What?"

"She made me swear not to tell you. Anyway, that's all settled now."

"Yes, I suppose it is."

"You're not disappointed, are you?"

"No, just acclimating to the arrangement."

"Yes, of course."

It was an odd feeling, to have severed ties with Sesbania. Or to have had her sever them. I'd known her for almost ten years, and had spent five just getting her in the sack. But I was used to taking things as they come. And, truth be told, it would have been difficult to adjust to her changeable nature after spending time with her far more agreeable counterpart.

I did have to wonder, however, about this secret she'd shared. She'd never shown much enthusiasm for sharing secrets. Likely as not, it was some sort of Parthian shot.

CHAPTER 9.

A RIVER TOO PECULIAR

The Orinoco flows west to east and ends in a delta some seventy miles wide. And like most river deltas, it's a web of narrow channels. But along the southern edge is a navigable stretch called the Rio Grande. It was this which we were hovering over when I emerged from my cabin.

There were five pairs of binoculars aboard. I recruited Clem, Mattie, Clio, and Liz to join me in scanning the river for the elusive seaplane. Women have far more of the patience necessary for such a task. And among the women aboard, these were the only ones congenial enough to approach.

Horatio had gone into his cabin for some bunk time, so it was Albertson at the helm. I instructed him to stay as near the center of the river as possible, and, as long as I provided him a course correction every twenty or thirty seconds, there seemed a reasonable chance he could pull it off.

At first, there were a good many false alarms—various watercraft, large wading birds, and what looked like a capybara wallowing in the shallows. But then Liz drew the others a fairly accurate depiction of a seaplane—along with a canoe, egret, and capybara to illustrate scale. She was quite the draftswoman. And, for a girl coming from her social milieu, surprisingly well acquainted with the anatomy of giant rodents.

The sun burned bright and we made excellent time. About two hours into the search, I spotted a city I deduced from my atlas was Ciudad Guayana, and an hour later, Ciudad Bolívar. At the time, Liz and Clio were looking forward from the bow end of the control room, while Clem and Mattie scanned to port and starboard, respectively. Horatio had returned to the helm, so I took position at a window in the mess from which I could scan to our stern. The idea being that at least three sets of eyes would look upon every bit of riverbank.

We passed any number of warehouses which might have harbored a plane. But there was no way of finding the thing if it wasn't out in the open. We just had to hope that luck would be on our side. And that Letitia hadn't been talking through her hat.

We ate at our posts and were still at it come early evening. From my vantage, *Lucy*'s shadow now appeared to follow us, moving from one bank to the other as the river twisted and turned. It struck me as unusually large, but I attributed that to the acute angle of the sun. That is, until it briefly diverged into two distinct shapes.

At first I thought it a trick of the eyes. Then I called to Horatio and had him make a quick turn to the north. There was no doubt about it. A second ship was traveling between us and the sun, and matching our course, turn for turn.

What had become by then a familiar feeling of dread fell over me as various possibilities ran through my head. Was it the mad Bonnet, seeking his promised rematch with his wayward daughters? Or the Cyclops, bent on reclaiming Clem and wreaking his vengeance on E. Pluribus? Or perhaps some new, uniquely riparian, pirate menace, waiting until we reached the depths of the jungle to strike with his own fiendishly clever armament—say, catapulted capybaras—and thereby send us crashing into Godknowswhat kind of steamy tropical reception. Just at that moment, I espied a thirty-foot anaconda sunbathing below. Its midsection was noticeably distended—about the size of a man, I calculated.

I had Horatio return to the center of the river, but there was no way our maneuver had gone unnoticed. I went myself up to the crow's nest and from there saw, silhouetted against the sun, a giant ship—larger even than Bonnet's. I suspected it was *The Midnight Sun*, but had Liz come up and confirm it.

"Marpesia's played that trick before. But why is she after us?"

"Well, I have a theory. Remember you told me that due to some mechanical difficulty, she could no longer pass from one world to the other?"

"Oh.... So you think maybe *she* needs this seaplane as much as you do?"

"Yes. Passing over requires a speed the steam ships aren't capable of. Maybe she somehow acquired aircraft engines to assist with that phase, and now needs replacements."

"I suppose that makes sense. But how did she find out about *this* seaplane? Or that it's up the Orinoco?"

"Last night, in Port of Spain, Clem happened to meet up with Sesbania. She told her of my plans to return to the real world and asked if Sesbania planned to return with me. No, was her reply, and she gave Clem her blessing to go in her stead. Anyway, Clem mentioned the seaplane."

"Oh. And having been much-wronged, Orithyia no doubt relayed that information to Marpesia, her... captain. I suppose you ought to see that as hopeful."

"How so?"

"Well, if her intention was to foil your attempt to go

back, it might mean you still have a chance to make amends.... Though, on the other hand, perhaps *she* plans on going back and hopes to leave *you* behind."

"I think that may be the more likely scenario."

"Yes. Well, she is much-wronged, isn't she?"

"That all depends on your perspective. You take a rather biased view on the subject."

"Umm."

"Do you think Marpesia's aware that we're aware?"

"Probably. She doesn't miss much. But I doubt she'll make a move before the plane's been located. Then it's fudge for us...."

"What about *her* vulnerabilities?"

"Can't think of any. Unless it's the way she allows her hatred of men to sometimes cloud her judgment."

"How exactly does that manifest itself?"

"Ahh... Well, you don't really want to know.... Trust me."

"Glad to." Regrettably, my imagination had no trouble filling in the details. "It will be dark soon and we'll need to call off the search until morning. No reason to mention this to the others. Might as well let someone sleep easy."

"All right.... I wonder what Reynard's preparing for supper?"

Apparently, she wasn't feeling too anxious herself. My fears, however, ably took up the slack. After seeing to the mooring of the ship—and then emptying most of a bottle of brandy—I allowed Clem to coax me into bed. She'd had her two nights of excess, but could still call up that determined look about the eyes whenever she felt the need. And that night, she felt the need. It was as if she'd cast a spell on me. I soon forgot all about the seaplane. And the giant airship hovering over us... commanded by a man-hating Amazon with an immobilizing fudge at the ready. The anaconda with the bloated belly took a little longer.

Clem was feeling energetic, and there was a good deal of animated reshuffling that night. Much of the time I wasn't even sure which end was up. Which is why, I think, it took me so long to realize the ship was under way.

I dressed and went out to the control room. Avarice was manning the helm alone.

"What are you doing?"

"You promised we'd stop at any cities we passed over, so I could look for franchisees. Now I find out you skipped at least two sizable ones."

"We can hit them on the way back."

"*My* priorities have precedence."

"How'd you manage to get the ship under way?"

"Sent a plate of three pastries upstairs, of course...."

"Look, we have to turn back!"

"Why? What is this secret mission you can't reveal, even to your own wife?"

"Well, it's rather complicated. Stop the ship and I'll tell you."

"Sorry. Not tempting enough."

"What if I tell you it involves a profit margin that dwarfs even that of pelican-themed barrooms catering to pirates...."

"Go on."

I told her everything. Being semi-mythical herself, she had no trouble grasping the concept of two worlds. And, being the personification of greed, no trouble appreciating the implications for profitable trade between the two. All sorts of things probably varied in price, she reasoned. Finally, she brought the ship to a halt.

"If you hadn't kept all this from me, we could have been working together!"

It seemed bizarre getting a lecture on trust from a Mortal Sin. But I suppose she did have a point.

Unfortunately, she had no idea how far downriver she'd taken us, only that it had been about two and a half hours.

"We'll just have to reverse course for the same time—and deliver a fresh plate of pastries to the harem." A not very precise method of navigation, but all we had.

As soon as the sun rose, I reassembled my spotters. Then an hour later, we saw the black ship hovering far off to the west.

It struck me as odd they hadn't taken up the search again. But when we got closer, I could see that they had—and been successful. We arrived just in time to see them hoist a modest-size seaplane up into the giant ship's hold.

"What now?" Liz asked.

"I was hoping you'd have a suggestion."

"Only one choice, really—run for it. Before the fudge starts flying."

"What! *Run?* Are you mad?" My greedy wife wasn't keen on the idea. I'd painted a pretty tempting picture of the potential profits and she found it rather difficult to abandon the tantalizing image.

Not surprisingly, given the danger, her crew mutinied. Albertson grabbed her from behind and, with Horatio's help, soon had her bound and gagged. She still managed to carry on something awful. So they next stuffed her into a canvas duffle and dragged her to the forward hold. There they suspended the sack from the ceiling.

All well and good for the present, but sooner or later someone was going to have to let her out.

II

I set a course for due north. I had no particular destination in mind, simply wanted to get out over open water as quickly as possible. The exotic forest below was giving me the creeps. We passed over the Venezuela coast about noon and I soon sighted the islands of Curaçao off to the west. Beyond that, the blue waters of the Caribbean stretched as far as the eye could see.

I'd be needing to set a new course for myself as well. The prospect of returning to the authentic world now seemed a distant one. But where to go? And what to do there? The truth was, I really had no marketable skills in either world. I'd so far gotten by on a mix of fast talking and unscrupulous scheming, but where would that leave Clem? And what about those troublesome wives of mine—five of them deadly by definition, and only one of those currently subdued?

Thirty minutes on, my reverie was cut short when I noticed a large land mass interrupting what should have been open sea. I checked the compass, then took a reading with the sextant. There was no doubt about it, Cousin Emmie had once more left her mark. I opened the atlas to the spread showing the Caribbean and there saw the bulk of that sea taken up by a pencil-drawn outline of a huge island: Madagascar.

We now passed a mere hundred feet above a forest even more exotic than that along the Orinoco, and containing even more exotic fauna. But at least not so threatening—a lemur, I suspect, would be far easier to evade than an anaconda.

I was exchanging bug-eyed looks with one of these curious prosimians when Avarice made her reappearance. Clem had taken pity on her and cut her down. The Sin's time in the duffle had taken a further toll on her normally alluring exterior—and an even greater one on her normally disagreeable manner. She was spitting fire. She spat fire even in the best of moods, so you can imagine how hot and fast it came now.

"Don't blame me," I told her. "It was *your* crew that mutinied."

"It was *you* who took on that... that *ullage* in the first place. Why is it no one aboard this damn ship can be trusted?"

"You mean, trusted to stay corrupted?"

"Don't twist my words!"

"I don't need to. Look, we all have our disappointments to live with. Let's just try to make the best of things."

"Best of things? How?"

"Well, we're currently passing over Madagascar. It seems to me there was a pirate port somewhere there. Maybe we could find a franchisee."

"That's an idea. Or better yet, go on to Port Royal. Father received an inquiry from a woman there that I never showed him."

"Sounds promising. Provided Port Royal is where it should be."

"Of course it's where it should be. Where else would it be? The island of Jamaica, just north of Madagascar."

"Yes, how silly of me. Now why don't you go and

take a nice bath. I'll let you know when we arrive."

"All right. I think I will.... But no tricks?"

"No tricks."

She smiled at me. And not even derisively. I marveled at my ability to placate her, and wondered then if there might not be some way to come to terms with my bizarre situation. What would be so horrible about running a string of profitable barrooms from the sky, accompanied by seven occasionally agreeable wives and one very agreeable consort? If nothing else, my sex life had become markedly more active. Markedly more dangerous as well, but one must take the bad with the good.

Fictional Port Royal had a very eighteenth-century air about it. And I'm not speaking only about the inadequate drainage, but the general ambience. While not strictly a pirate port, it was known to be very accommodating to members of that profession. And privateers even more so. The key, if I remembered my lore correctly, was to stay on the good side of the royal governor. I mentioned this to Avarice and suggested we visit him with some gifts. She proposed bestowing her sisters, Sloth, Envy, and Melpomene.

"Frankly, I doubt that would net us much goodwill."

"I suppose you're right. Then why not throw in the vine as well?"

"No, she'd likely object. But why not something that will make him irresistible to the lady already sharing his bed?"

"Like what?"

"Indoor plumbing."

"Indoor plumbing?"

"Yes, I think Liz wouldn't mind settling down, and where she goes, Percival goes...."

"Well, I suppose his work's done here. All right. But couldn't we at least throw in Envy as well?"

"I think she might jinx the deal. Let me go consult with Liz."

As I expected, she'd been thinking herself of how to exit our unconventional circle.

"I don't want to sound puritanical, but this really isn't the ideal environment to raise children in."

"Children?"

"Yes. You know what those are, don't you? ...I'd be surprised if you don't have a few on the way as well...."

"As well? Does that mean you're..."

"Knocked up? Yes. Percival's very excited."

"And you?"

"Oh, I'm game.... Do you think this governor will hire us on?"

"You can bet his wife will."

The next morning, the four of us—Avarice, myself, and the prospective parents—all went down together. We met with the lady of the house and the deal was sealed in a matter of minutes. As it happened, the governor and his missus had three teenage daughters.

Percival and family were provided a salary and bungalow with a view, and we a charter to open a taproom "for the comfort and entertainment of seamen, whatever their ilk or inclinations may be." Obligingly vague enough to include pirates and, I'm afraid, their predilection for pelicans.

Next we located the woman who'd sent Bonnet the query. It turned out she already operated a house for the comfort and entertainment of seamen, whatever their ilk or inclinations may be. And from the glimpse we caught in the anteroom, that whatever was all-inclusive.

We were told by a servant that the lady herself was engaged. On his own initiative, he took us to a veranda and there served us a light lunch while we waited. Given that she seemed to be doing quite well on her own, I wondered aloud if this woman really needed a franchise.

"Oh, you underestimate the drawing power of the Pelican trademark," Avarice told me. "Pirates seem to have a visceral reaction to it."

"Yes, I've noticed. Poor birds."

The door of an inner room opened, but instead of the lady of the house entering, it was a man. And you'll never guess who....

Well, all right. You probably guessed immediately who: Jack.

"What are you doing here?" I asked, somewhat needlessly.

"Maybe I should be asking you."

I introduced Avarice, and gave him a brief précis of our business there.

"Could work," he said. Though it wasn't entirely clear if he was speaking of the franchise scheme, or my wife, whom he was surveying over a wry smile.

I won't say I was surprised. Her wounds had mostly healed by then, and she was wearing a rather flattering silk blouse over a skirt just long enough to leave something to mystery. What *did* surprise me was the coy expression with which she answered him. By merely walking into the room, Jack had made another conquest.

I suppose I should've been grateful a husband's evisceration hadn't been necessary. But I couldn't help feeling a tinge of jealousy. Jack's company had a way of quickly wearing thin.

"Well, I gotta be going," he told us. "Still tryin' to run down that friend of mine."

"Eugenia?"

"Yeah—you haven't come across her again, have you?"

"No, sorry. Had a mission up the Orinoco."

"Whose Orinoco?"

Jack and his new disciple laughed together. Then she whispered—under her breath, yet clearly for his benefit—"Not mine, certainly."

He gave her a wink and was gone.

She was still staring after him, open-mouthed, when an oddly attractive woman of about thirty entered the room. If she had a doppelganger back in the real world, I certainly hadn't met her—because I would definitely have remembered if I had. On the left side, her hair was cut close—no further than her ear—but fell in a cascade of waves to her right shoulder. An unusual look. But not nearly so unusual as its color—peach, I would call it. She wore a loose-fitting shift, which mostly obscured her figure—save the two shapely legs extending below and the two contented nipples acting as bowsprits. She was as gracious as she was intriguing, and in no time at all we came to an arrangement.

"Now let us consummate the deal," she said directly to me. "With a drink, I mean."

She and I laughed, while Avarice looked on with something akin to hostility. Turnabout may be fair play, generally speaking—but *not* to a Mortal Sin.

We made our way back to *Lucy* both lost to our thoughts. It had been a fruitful day, and one not lacking in surprises. But there was one more yet to come....

III

Aggie was back aboard. To say I was shocked to see her would be a supreme understatement. The ornery scribe had never missed an opportunity to make clear her low opinion of me. I've a pretty thick skin—and, I'll admit, need one. But that little sheba could always manage to get under it.

She'd been chatting with Horatio and Mattie. At her feet was the carpetbag she'd left with.

"I thought we'd seen the last of you." It came out a little more acerbic than I'd intended, but nothing like the acid she usually splashed about.

"Sorry. I didn't think you'd mind." She sounded defensive, almost sheepish.

"No, I don't mind. You're welcome anytime. Just grab a hammock. Had enough of Jack?"

"You aren't kidding I've had enough of him."

I don't like to toot my own horn—oh, what the hell, I like nothing better. Still, you have to admit I called this one right. Way back when, I predicted that when Aggie finally fell, she'd fall hard [Ed. note: see Book One]. And this, apparently, was exactly what happened.

"Come on, you need a drink." I took her up to the library. There were still a few crates of rum Clio hadn't unpacked yet. It was inferior stuff, but I suspected Aggie wasn't feeling particularly choosy. A note on the door informed us the librarian was off to the bathhouse, but visitors were welcome to come in.

Aggie drained three shots in the time it took me to finish one.

"What a son of a bitch," she said.

"Jack? An acquired taste, certainly. Were you

caught off guard by the sleeping arrangements?"

"No, I'd heard about that."

"You just didn't expect to care?"

"Yeah. Maybe that's it. What a son of a bitch."

Thus ended the first bottle.

In an effort to distract her, I told her all about my own adventures since we'd left each other's company. It had only been a week or so, but a busy one. There was the coming and going of Sesbania; the going and coming of Clem; the revelations in Nassau; my heroic battle with the Cyclops; the Sins' overpowering of their father, and the liberation of the Limnads; Lafitte's surprising me in bed; the exit of our quarrelsome saucier (though I withheld Reynard's disclosure that we'd been served her friend, the parrot); the Limnads masquerading as Sins; our conversation with Letitia, the taciturn burro; and finally, the misadventure up the Orinoco.

"Whose Orinoco?" She was halfway into the second bottle by then, and the words came not so clearly.

"I'll leave that to your imagination."

"Hah! Come here...." she slurred.

When I demurred, she stumbled to her feet and fell into my lap. After throwing her arms around me, she planted a wet kiss on my lips—then promptly passed out.

I carried her to Clio's cot and kissed her goodnight on the forehead.

That was about three in the afternoon. After supper, I went up with some coffee, sandwiches, and aspirin.

"How's the patient?" I asked my favorite Muse.

"I may have heard a moan a minute ago. For your information, symposia are permitted in the library, even encouraged—but common courtesy demands the librarian be invited."

"Sorry, this symposium was a bit of an emergency."

"Ah. Unrequited love…"

"How'd you guess?"

"To be honest, it was Melpomene's supposition. I came upon her sniffing the air—she can smell a tormented soul at five thousand cubits."

"Five thousand cubits?"

"Well, Roman cubits."

We heard another moan. I carried over my tray of offerings and found Aggie raised upon her elbows cautiously shaking her head.

"What happened?"

"You met a bottle of rum and it swept you off your feet."

"Jesus H. Christ. What kinda rotgut ya serve 'round here?"

Earlier, she seemed to have weaned herself from the obligatory vernacular. But apparently that was just a passing phase.

She took the aspirin and downed them with coffee. However, she steered well clear of the sandwiches—given her circumstances, egg salad might not have been the wisest choice.

"Hey, was that all true, what ya told me?"

"Of course… but are you referring to anything in particular?"

"About that broad in Nassau, being able to go back and forth to the real world."

"Well, I haven't witnessed it. But it would account for her exalted position there. She calls it her fiefdom. And there has to be some way of doing it besides a random storm, or *The Midnight Sun* wouldn't have been able to go snatch the women off of the *Paris*."

"Shit. I been in pipe dreams that weren't so nutty. How about the airplane engines? Does that part make sense?"

"Make sense? That'd be aiming a little high. Let's say, within the realm of possibility given the context we find ourselves in."

"Christ. Yer soundin' like a lawyer again.... What about that heap we came on?"

"Wilbur? Blown to bits...."

"Yeah, I know. But Cartwright told me you caught those islanders scavengin' parts *before* it got blown to bits."

"He's right.... I'd forgotten all about that. They seemed pretty haphazard about it, but who knows.... I may owe you one, Aggie."

"Then get me aboard."

"Get you aboard?"

"Yeah. I got a hell of a story to file."

"Yes. All right." I'd only been promised two spots, but we were still dealing in hypotheticals at that point.

"Thanks," she said—and even sounded like she meant it.

I told Avarice the promising news. Needless to say, she derided me for not having thought of it earlier. It was dark by then, and we'd played the plate-of-three-pastries gambit too many times for it to be effective anymore. Both her sisters and the pastry supply were for the time being depleted. We'd have to wait until the next morning to set course for the Bahamas.

She looked to be in one of her moods, and I half-expected her to invite me into her chamber. But that wasn't it. It was some sort of trance. She just stared into space, wearing an enigmatic smile. I wondered if she was thinking of Jack. Then, however, I noticed her lips moving with her thoughts—she was calculating the future returns on her new investment.

Though it wasn't even nine o'clock, Clem was already fast asleep. Feeling restless myself, I took the opportunity to check on Aggie. She'd once again taken up the bottle—and her grievances with Jack. Melpomene was there, feigning commiseration, but in truth merely egging the scribe on for her own satisfaction.

"You poor thing. Don't hold back, tell me all...."

Annoyed by both Aggie's slurred protestations and her sister's intrusion, the normally friendly Clio snapped at me for leaving my lost puppy at her door.

"How am I supposed to get any work done with this going on?"

When I suggested she and I go find a secluded nook, she flung *The Complete Works of Dickens*, Volume III, at me. Then she blamed *me* for her treatment of the book. So much for my reasonable Muse.

I went back down and crawled in next to Clem. Still asleep, she emitted a sound of vague contentment and then lay her arm over me. One thing was certain: if I needed to make a choice regarding which of my consorts to hang onto, it would be an easy one.

About five the next afternoon we sighted Andros Island. Wilbur's unfortunate immolation had charred a large area of brush, so the site of his demise was easy to locate. I brought *Lucy* down just a little ways up the beach. Once moored, I suggested the wives and crew remain aboard to guard the ship.

"No. I'm coming with you," Avarice insisted.

"Suit yourself. But there's a good chance the engines have been rendered useless and our reception will be a hostile one. I'm sure they'd like nothing better than to disassemble *Lucy* as they did Wilbur."

She looked at me suspiciously. And not without reason. Had I really thought that the case, I'd be the last one to leave the ship. Nonetheless, while Aggie, Clem, and I went off to the village to enter negotiations, my acquisitive wife stayed safely behind.

"Your engines?" the headman asked. I assumed he was playing dumb, but Clem correctly deduced that it was the terminology that confused him. So I described the machines in detail.

"Ah, those fans of yours!"

The only use the villagers could find for an aircraft engine was to create a breeze. They used them on nights when the air was still and humid. Within a month, however, they'd run out of gasoline.

"You can run them on rum—but better to be hot *with* rum than cool without it."

"You speak with the wisdom of a true leader," I told him.

They'd only been able to scavenge three of Wilbur's engines. But these they agreed to sell for ten British pounds and five cases of rum. For an additional shilling, I arranged to have them simulate an attack on *Lucy*.

We watched as they put on a spirited show, sending up a miscellany of missiles, and then setting the mooring ropes on fire. As I expected, my changeable wives and pliable crew wasted no time in making their exit.

Both Clem and Aggie seemed shocked by my de facto divorcement. Many people, perhaps women particularly, have a partiality for convention—even when it's nothing more than a veneer masking something wholly unconventional. Sesbania was the same in that regard.

"Look," I said. "They never had much use for me—even less so now that their father's signed over the franchise business."

"I suppose.... But what about Horatio, and Albertson?" Clem asked.

"What about them? They'd thrown me over days ago. No, my adventures as an airship privateer are over. They'll need to learn to get by without me. I'll be living the quiet life from now on. Maybe even cash in by writing my memoirs: *E. Pluribus Van Slyke, Airship Privateer*. Has a nice ring to it."

"Listen, ya gink, try ta jump my scoop and I'll be wearin' yer family jewels on a string," Aggie explained. "Savvy?"

"Sure, Aggie." Why hadn't I left her behind with the others?

Given the headman's loose interpretation of property rights, I was afraid to let the engines out of my sight even for a moment. I strung my hammock beside them and built a fire. Clem had her own hammock nearby, but just as we were about ready to hit the sack, that look came over her. I pointed out the awkwardness of sleeping together in a hammock.

"Who needs a hammock? The sand is plenty soft."

Well, a woman able to muster that determined look at will can be pretty persuasive. In no time, she had me at work. And she seemed pleased with how things were progressing—but only up until the initial bite of a sand flea. When she first cried, "Ow!" I thought I'd neglected to shave that morning. With the second cry, she reached a hand down to massage her bum; there'd been an assault on her baggage train. By the third cry, her enthusiasm for sleeping on the beach had been squelched quite effectively.

Her ardor, however, showed no signs of flagging. Quite the contrary. Whether some aphrodisiacal property accompanies the pain of a sand flea's bite, I can't say. But her look had taken on a wildness I'd not noticed before. What's more, it turned out she knew some very creative ways for using a hammock to advantage, making a positive virtue of necessity.

And that's not my opinion alone. When we at last fell quiet, exhausted, a short round of applause came from just beyond the light of the fire. We accepted their recognition affably, as good manners required; but Clem insisted we decline the curtain call.

CHAPTER 10.

HOME IS WHERE THEY CAN'T CATCH YOU

At first light, I attended to the next order of business: getting word to Gertie. I hired a fishing smack to make the trip to Nassau. But still wary of leaving the engines unguarded, I sent Aggie in my stead. She'd had prior dealings with Gertie and I felt fairly sure I could trust her. Which is about as far as I'm congenitally able to trust anyone.

Clem and I spent a lazy day swimming, napping, and whatnot. Then about eight that evening, Aggie returned with positive news: help would be arriving that night.

It was well after midnight when we awoke to the familiar chugga-chugga and watched as an airship moored just off the beach. Gertie descended with a sum of hard currency, five cases of rum, and a dozen scruffy henchmen. The moment payment had been rendered, the work of winching the engines aboard the ship commenced.

"How is it possible you forgot about these?" Gertie asked.

"Well, as you may remember, in the days after our landing I had a few other things on my mind, such as my trial and your sentencing me to be abandoned at sea."

"Oh, yes. Thank you for reminding me of that. With no frying pan, if I recall." She smiled, but a smile which combined the ambiguity of the Mona Lisa's with the amused contempt of a Mortal Sin's. Sesbania deployed it frequently. "Are you sure they'll fit my plane?"

"Don't worry. We'll get them to fit."

"But there's only three.... The plane has four."

"Minor problem."

Once the engines were secured, we all returned to Nassau. There, Gertie asked me to her office in order to confer.

"You only mentioned one other passenger besides yourself. Yet both these women seem to think they're coming along."

"No chance I could arrange an extra passage?"

"No room. I need to bring a consignment to Miami."

"Well, don't worry. I'll work it out."

"Yes, I'm sure you will."

For a moment, I thought she was envisaging that I'd spend what was left of that night with her. But on closer examination, I realized she hadn't been flirting; and her remark wasn't meant as a compliment.

"You better get some sleep. You have a lot of work ahead of you."

"Yes. Goodnight."

She was right about the work. Getting the Italian engines mounted on her plane took five of us a full week. However, that was just the first of the complications.

Had they been more powerful than the American Liberties they were replacing, we might have gotten by with just the three. But they were appreciably *less* powerful. So the next day we disassembled the four worn-out Liberties. By mixing parts, we were able to come up with one that ran consistently—not consistently well, but consistently.

That evening, I gave Gertie the news that her plane

was airworthy. *Probably* airworthy would have been more accurate, but I've always been economical in my use of adverbs.

"Good, so there shouldn't be any problem."

"Well, one small problem. It won't be able to carry quite the same load."

"Then someone will need to stay behind. I need every bit of space for the booze.... If you want to know the truth, I'm nearly broke."

"Then what if I let Aggie take my place? That will knock off close to a hundred pounds."

"All right.... If that's what you want."

I have a way of backing into noble acts without giving them much thought. But in this case, there were some genuine doubts motivating me. First, I didn't really feel up to betraying Aggie's trust. I know she was an infuriating little cuss. But she was an infuriating little cuss in a kind of sisterly way. And don't forget, it was she who bought my freedom when I was destined to be marooned on the Sargasso without a frying pan [Ed. note: see Book One]. Yes, I know, it was using the jewels she stole from my own hoard. Still, not every girl would have made that sacrifice.

And then there was Clem. Without me in tow, she stood a much better chance of securing the countess's affection, and thereby her fortune. But in all honesty, there was something else, something not so selfless. Clem's devotion to me was just a little *too* unconditional. Since I could never measure up to the same standard, the result was a perpetual feeling of guilt.

My relationship with Sesbania was far more equitable, incorporating as it did a healthy amount of mutual mistrust. And though I might never see *her* again, I could easily imagine coming to like terms with the equally mistrustful Gertie. Life could be very comfortable, if nominally fictional, as her consort.

If you're keeping score, I feel I deserve partial credit for this noble act—even if it didn't come to pass. The next morning, Aggie approached me bearing a thick envelope.

"I'm not goin' back. Least not yet."

"What about your Pulitzer?"

"Ah... ishkabibble," she said, but without the usual enthusiasm. "Take this to my editor. Maybe I'll win it in absentia."

I didn't press her further. However, I felt sure she was making the wrong choice. I could think of only one reason she wanted to stay, and it wasn't a good one. Lots of women make the mistake of falling for a man already taken. But Jack was a case unto himself. Not only did he have his in-house harem, he had paramours sprinkled about all the better pirate ports.

On a positive note, with neither Aggie nor me aboard, Gertie would be able to carry another hundred pounds of liquor. Or so I thought. During a test run later that morning, we discovered the plane had even less lift than I'd estimated. Dombrowski adjusted the engines to achieve the maximum horsepower, but the hotter temperatures would take a toll.

"I doubt she'll be good for more than one trip," he told me. "Then she'll need a complete overhaul—and probably four new engines."

I relayed this news to Gertie. She didn't look pleased.

"That changes everything.... I *must* have a working seaplane. I'll need to take all the liquor I can, and buy another plane. Your friends will need to take their chances. Maybe there'll be another trip. What do you think is the least I can expect to spend on a replacement?"

"Haven't a clue. Thousands, certainly. And it wouldn't have anything near the capacity of this one. The NC class is unique, and there aren't many of them around."

"Damn."

"How'd you come by this plane?"

"It belonged to a rum-runner friend. I was his pilot, and...." A blush concluded her sentence. "Well, one afternoon I caught him in bed with...." This time, it was an ink bottle thrown at a mirror. Once calm, she continued: "I took off for parts unknown. In my anger I pushed the plane beyond its rated speed, and on landing, found myself here."

"So, in a nutshell, you stole it."

"Technically, yes."

"Well, you might be able to come by another the same way. And of the same class."

"Steal it? From whom?"

"The U.S. Navy. I saw one in Pensacola a few months back."

"Do you think we could get away with it?"

"We?"

"Of course, we.... I'd make it worth your while."

"All right, why not? We'll need Dombrowski along, too. He knows the base there better than I do. It will mean no liquor this trip."

"There's not much point in taking over the booze if I can't get back. We'll just have to risk it."

The next morning we were off. Our plan was to fly

straight to Pensacola and snatch the plane P.D.Q. During the flight, I learned there was more to crossing over than mere speed. Thirty miles out, Gertie took the plane to near its maximum flying altitude—then nosedived toward the sea.

About a hundred yards from impact, she pulled up. I now knew that her insistence that we forgo breakfast had nothing to do with weight, and that she'd been feeling more than simple anger during her first trip over. For the remainder of the flight, she avoided looking in my direction. She'd deduced that I had deduced, and it obviously made her uncomfortable for me to be privy to her moment of despondency.

Ten miles short of the Florida coast, the first engine went. Then a mile later, the second one. We landed just off Miami Beach with only one working engine. The Coast Guard met us, no doubt expecting to find the plane packed with booze. While they made a futile search, we waded ashore.

Gertie suggested a hotel on the far side of town, where we could remain inconspicuous. But I felt in need of some indulging. I chose the Flamingo. After leaving the others in the little café, I went to the desk and informed the clerk we were with Noyes Congdon's party.

"He'll be arriving tomorrow. Sorry for the short notice. Do you think you can find three rooms for us?"

"Part of Mr. Congdon's party? Of course.... But he's already arrived."

"Oh." That was one eventuality I hadn't considered. "He must have caught an earlier train."

The clerk tilted his head toward the elevator lobby. "There's Mr. Congdon now."

"Ah. Ideal."

In the café, I gave Dombrowski his room key and Clem ours.

"Where's Gertie?"

"Said she needed to make a phone call."

They went off just as Gertie reappeared. She looked worried.

"What's wrong?"

"Oh, nothing. But I have some business here in Miami I need to look after. I'll have to meet you in Pensacola, say, a week from today."

"That suits me. I wanted to head north to settle a few things anyway."

Congdon entered the bar as I was speaking. He looked as if he'd seen a ghost.

"I... I never thought... Well, we heard you were lost at sea...."

"Mere rumor." I introduced him to Gertie. But they were both too absorbed by their own thoughts to take much notice of each other.

"Were you, by any chance... successful?" he asked me.

"Yes, I learned what happened to the women. And how it happened. But it's a little too involved to go into now."

"Then you found Lizzie?"

"I did, yes. But I have some bad news there."

"Not—dead?" He didn't say it with quite the alarm one would expect of a devoted fiancé.

"Ah, no. I guess there's no easy way to put it: she's married a steamfitter named Percival and they're living in Port Royal."

"Oh. Port Royal?"

"Jamaica. But don't bother writing. I hope you aren't too devastated."

"On the contrary, I couldn't be happier—for her, I mean. Well, and me.... Do you remember that girl you introduced me to?"

"Kate?"

"That's right. Well, one thing led to another...."

"Yes... I thought it might. Is she here with you?"

"Oh, no. She's out in Reno. I'm here on some business." He lowered his voice to a whisper: "Real estate."

At the mention of those two words, Gertie became attentive. "Did you say real estate?"

"Yes, values here are going through the roof," he told her. He looked about as if not wanting to be overheard. "If you'll take my advice, you'll put every dime you can get hold of into Florida property. I am. Everything."

As it happened, I didn't have a dime to put into Florida real estate. Which, as it turned out, was just as well. By the end of the conversation, Gertie had her arm wrapped around his and insisted he dine with us later that evening.

The meal was a dull affair, Congdon going on about the planned hotels, golf courses, spas, etc., and Gertie seeming to eat it up. She was up to something. As soon as we could escape, Clem and I went for a walk on the beach.

"I'm going to drop you off with a friend in Washington for a week or so. I need to come back down here to help Gertie get that plane."

"Does this friend know Sesbania?"

"Yes. It will give you a chance to practice being her. We'll tell him you have amnesia."

"Him?"

"Name's Baker, Ross Baker. Went to Annapolis with me. Nice fellow. In fact... No, I probably shouldn't tell you...."

"Tell me what?"

"Well, back in the day, Sesbania had an enormous crush on him."

"Really? Is he good-looking?"

"I suppose some people might think so."

Yes, I too was up to something. Having already decided to go back with Gertie, I thought I might as well leave Clem in as comfortable a position as possible. In truth, Sesbania had found my old school chum too forward. It was *he* who had the crush. But the power of suggestion being what it is, I thought there might be a chance to stoke the furnace.

II

The next morning at breakfast, Congdon took me aside.

"Do you... Do you think you'll see Lizzie again?"

"Good chance of it."

"I don't want to embarrass her. But ask her to consider this a wedding present."

He handed me five one-hundred-dollar bills.

"I don't think she'll mind," I assured him—not that there was much chance of her ever seeing it.

I wired Baker just before Clem and I boarded the train north. The next evening he met us at Union Station, flowers in hand. He had a little place up the Potomac. I suggested we have supper in town before heading there, but he demurred.

"Oh, the woman who keeps house for me put out some sandwiches."

"That would suit me," Clem (now in her role as Sesbania) told him.

It was a hot, still night, as Washington summer nights are wont to be. We ate on his terrace. Then Clem went in to take a bath and Baker brought out a bottle of Scotch.

"You'll find Sesbania has forgotten quite a bit of her past. Couldn't remember you at all, in fact."

"So I noticed. Well, maybe that's just as well," he joked.

"Maybe. The important thing is to take it slow."

"Take what slow?"

"Well, reacquainting her with things."

"Of course. But can't you tell me what happened?"

"Only she can do that.... Though it may be erased from her memory completely."

"Must have been horribly traumatic."

"Yes. She's in need of friends now."

"Don't worry about that. How long do you expect to be in Florida?"

"Oh, not long.... Just long enough to steal a seaplane."

"Steal a seaplane?"

"Yes. One of the NCs from Pensacola."

"Good God. What for?"

"I'm going into business with some rum-runners."

"Sounds a little risky, doesn't it?"

"Maybe. But I don't have much choice."

"They're blackmailing you?"

"Yes.... That's it exactly. I can't explain now. But should something happen, and I don't make it back..."

"You can count on me. You know I'll look after her."

"Good. That's all I wanted to hear. I'll be going to New York first thing in the morning, and won't have time to stop on my way back down."

"Well, that's probably for the best—and you ought to keep a low profile until catching your train."

"What do you mean?"

"The Navy's investigating you again. They say you lost your ship through gross negligence."

"But it wasn't even their ship when it went down! We bought it."

"Yes, but the crew were Navy men, and you were wearing the uniform...."

"Is Gilbert behind this?"

"Him and some others. Trying to deflect blame over the fiasco of buying that misbegotten ship in the first place. Stay out of sight, and it will probably blow over."

"Gilbert must know I helped Kate escape from him."

"You did?"

"Yes. She's out in Reno, waiting for a divorce so she can marry Congdon."

"Congdon? Hit the big time, did she? But what exactly happened to you? And Sesbania?"

"If I told you even half of it, you'd call me a liar."

"Well, you *are* a liar."

Given he wasn't going to believe me anyway, I went ahead and told him some of my adventures, including the night spent in the company of the twin redheads, Wrath and Pride. He wasn't as impressed as I expected.

"You know, I met those same two in Atlantic City, two summers ago, I think."

Braggart.

When Clem and I said our good-byes at the station

the next morning, she cried. I don't know if she suspected something, or was just feeling emotional. Anyhow, she deserved someone like Baker. Someone who'd adore her, and, having played football, was more accustomed to having his limbs dislocated.

Just before hopping on the train, I handed her a handkerchief to dry her tears, and told Baker not to let her out of his sight for the next hour or two.

The handkerchief was one of her own. Earlier that morning, I'd placed a few precious drops of the aphrodisiacal elixir on it. Yes, she'd had her two nights. Nonetheless, I imagine they had an interesting ride back up the Potomac—and don't ask me whose Potomac.

In New York, I took Aggie's story to her editor at the *World*, then waited while he read it.

"Jesus." He tossed the sheaf back at me. "She's hitting the pipe again, isn't she?"

"Having read her account on the train up, I can assure you it's all true."

"Aren't you the boob who was drummed out of the Navy for attacking a circus?"

"A simulated attack. And I wasn't drummed out, per se. Besides, that's not relevant. Look, can you come up with another explanation for the airship abduction of women from a steamship of the French Line?"

"We've got a whole slew better than this one: Arab white slavers, Chinese white slavers, Hebrew white slavers, Mexican white slavers—take your pick."

"I'd have thought Amazon pirates would trump all those."

"Oh, that part I can use. But they'll be *Oriental* Amazon pirates, or *African* Amazon pirates, not *fictional* Amazon pirates."

He drew out three hundred dollars for me to give Aggie.

"But tell her that's it. She can come see me after she sobers up."

From there, I went out to Brooklyn to visit Cousin Emmie. She cried on seeing me. It was one of the few times I remember seeing her cry. But mere seconds later, the tears of relief were vaporized by the heat of anger.

"You selfish ass! We heard you were dead. Is Sesbania all right?"

"Yes, she's fine. In fact, twice her normal self."

"What on earth does that mean? And why didn't you wire us?"

"Well, for the simple reason there's no reliable means of communication between your make-believe world and this one."

She started to admonish me for my choice of words, but I cut her off. Then began laying out the whole ludicrous tale before her.

"Did you really meet Jack Tigue?" She was genuinely excited at the news.

"Oh, yes. And his harem...."

"Harem?"

Things went downhill from there. By the time I got to my marriage ceremony, she'd taken on her customary mien and was emitting vague sounds of skepticism.

"*Mortal Sins?* ...Look, I don't like being teased. I suppose Harry put you up to this."

"It's all true, Emmie. I thought you'd be pleased. Here's the report of a trusted journalist." I handed her the envelope with Aggie's account. "It confirms your wild stories about visiting airships."

"The difference is *my* wild stories are all perfectly true. I don't know what you're up to, Pluribus, but I don't want to hear another word about it. Right now, you need to write your brother and sister."

She retrieved pen and paper, then sat by, reading Aggie's report and making sure I did as she'd instructed. The whole episode left me feeling like a child caught telling tales. Then husband Harry showed up and I had to suffer his ridicule on top of it.

When Emmie went into the kitchen, he poured me a drink.

"Better down this."

I looked at it suspiciously. "Poisoned?"

"No, you won't be getting off that easy. Your friend Rutledge just went belly up."

He handed me a newspaper. It was just as Aggie had told me back in Pensacola. Rutledge had bet big on credit and was now caught short.

"Skip to page three," he told me.

I did, and there saw how Rutledge blamed his condition on the theft of one hundred thousand dollars—by yours truly. Apparently, he was banking on my having been lost at sea.

"It's nonsense!"

"Uh-huh. Well, I suppose you'll get your day in court—assuming those creditors don't lynch you first."

"You won't mention this to Emmie."

"Not until after you leave. Which better be tonight."

"That was my plan."

Along with dessert, Emmie dished out another bit of disquieting news.

"I think you should know, there are some men looking for you."

"What men?"

"Oh, unpleasant men. And they sounded rather anxious to find you."

"Navy men?"

"Navy men? Heavens, no. More like... gangsters."

"Why would gangsters be looking for me?"

"Well, if I had to guess, I'd say they were in the employ of the countess."

"The countess?"

"Yes. You remember her: Sesbania's cunning and *very* devoted guardian."

"You forgot cold-blooded and merciless," Harry reminded her.

Emmie gave a vague little nod as if to confirm his amplification.

I decided to forgo a second helping of pie. The land of make-believe was calling me home....

I snuck out of town on a westbound sleeper, then turned south and spent an eventful night in New Orleans in the company of an old flame by the name of Louisa Cantrell. She couldn't have been a day under fifty, but Louisa had the joie de vivre of a seventeen-year-old girl. And so did the seventeen-year-old girl who shared the apartment with her.

Three days after leaving New York, I arrived in Pensacola to find Gertie in the hotel lounge enjoying a poorly disguised martini.

"Have one on me." She called the order to the waiter.

"You're looking chipper."

"Why not? I got out of a tough spot in the nick of time. And I have you to thank for it."

"You mean, this plane we're going after?"

"No. I mean introducing me to Congdon."

"He let you in on one of his real-estate ventures?"

"On the contrary."

"I don't follow you."

"Well, I've been buying up land in Miami for years. For my retirement. And all on credit. That phone call I made, just after we landed. It was to my lawyer. I told him I wanted to cash it all in now. He said it was probably too late...."

"Too late?"

"The bubble's about to burst and buyers are drying up."

"Ah—but not Congdon."

She laughed. I wouldn't call it a sinister laugh, exactly, but very close to it.

"How much did you clear?"

"Plenty. And I was wondering if it might not be safer for all concerned to buy the plane. Not legitimately, of course. But disperse enough to persuade the men involved to look the other way while we abscond with it."

"A noble thought. Unfortunately, I can say with some authority that your average naval officer isn't bribable."

"Really? Where do these people come from?"

"Oh, here and there. And the officer in charge of the seaplanes here is about as straitlaced as they come. Worse, he may feel he has a grievance with me...."

"His wife?"

"How'd you guess that?"

"*Please*. I'm not the naïf you might think."

Naïf wasn't the word I'd use to describe the rum-running queen of Nassau. But if she wanted to be thought of as a naïf, I was perfectly willing to go along.

As of then, this sojourn in the land of the real had involved more coincidences than a pulp magazine serial. But there were a few more yet to come. Sitting in a darkened corner of the room was a Navy lieutenant commander of my acquaintance named Erickson. The very man I'd alluded to a moment earlier. He was drinking a poorly disguised gin and tonic.

When he spotted me, he rose to his feet. I excused myself to Gertie, and went over to join him.

"My God. I never thought I'd see you again."

"Well, the news of my demise was somewhat premature—or whatever it was Twain said. But I'm just as surprised to see you in here. Being a little obvious, aren't you? Flouting the Constitution this way."

"Oh. Well, things aren't going too well." He fell back into his seat and I took one beside him. "Do you think anyone can tell?" he asked, staring at his glass.

"I think it pretty certain. What's not going well? Your career?" Perhaps there'd be a chance of bribing him after all. If not, there was always blackmail.

"My career? Oh, that's fine. I'm up for a post at the Navy Department. Should hear any day. No, it's my wife...."

"Oh... ah..."

"Anna... You've probably forgotten, but you met her in New Jersey."

"Oh, yes. Of course. Is she ill?"

"Well... She's moved out."

"Upset with you?"

"Not exactly. She's... I don't know why I'm telling you this.... Promise not to repeat it?"

"Of course I won't repeat it."

"She's moved into an apartment... with a young nurse. A girl named Alice something. And there are rumors...."

"Oh. And it wouldn't look good for your career if those rumors circulated more widely."

"Yes. But that's not the important thing. I want Anna back. But she won't even talk to me. What could she see in this girl?"

"I have a theory.... You know, it might be possible to tempt her back, depending on how wedded she is to her new arrangement."

"What do you have in mind?"

"Well, first off, you need to figure out if there's something this girl is providing that you didn't."

"I can think of a few things...."

"Yes, but you aren't without assets yourself."

"Maybe she's not interested in those anymore."

"Maybe. But there is a way for you to make sure."

Yes, I had a plan. However, it first required giving him a thorough lesson in female anatomy. I tried getting it across via detailed description. But so thoroughly ignorant was he of his wife's finer points, he had trouble grasping the gist of the thing. Just as he had hers. So that night, I contacted an old friend, Obligin' Nell.

III

Nell was never shy about displaying her anatomy to strangers, and by the time we left her company, Erickson knew just exactly what was where.

"But you think it's necessary to use... Well... to..."

"Yes, emphatically necessary," I told him. "At least in my experience."

"Well, I suppose this does help. But why have you gone to the trouble?"

My answer didn't shock him quite as much as you might think it would. After all, he *did* know my record.

At his house the next evening, we laid out plans for the operation in detail. Erickson would be on duty the following night, so that was when we'd strike. First, I would send a couple bottles of second-rate hooch to the guardhouse about eleven. Then he would come by and order the inebriates on some unpleasant detail as punishment for drunkenness. Next, we'd come up by boat, knock him out—or at least make it look that way—and take off in the seaplane.

"What kind of shape is it in?"

"Just overhauled. Listen, when you knock me out, make it look good. It has to be convincing."

Things went about as well as they could. Dombrowski delivered the hooch to the guardhouse. Then half an hour later, he, Gertie, and I boarded a hired dinghy and quietly approached the dock where the NC was moored. Erickson was there waiting.

"Remember, make it look good," he said.

"Don't worry about that. But first, give me your handkerchief."

"My handkerchief?"

"Yes, quickly."

He did, and like the little Cupid I'd become, I scented it with what looked to be the last three drops of perfume.

"Tomorrow, when your wife comes to visit you in the hospital—"

"Hospital?"

"You want it to look good, don't you?"

"Yes, all right. But how do you know she'll come?"

"Odds are she won't be able to help herself. Anyway, when she does, you make sure she gets a good whiff of this. Good-bye, Erickson.... All right, Dombrowski, he's all yours...."

I've never taken much joy in beating a man, especially one who hadn't offended me. But give an enlisted man a chance at knocking about an officer without penalty, and you've made his day.

"Well, I guess it's good-bye," Gertie said, extending me her hand.

"Actually, I was planning on going back with you. If that berth's still open."

"Oh. Have you gotten all your wives, and would-be wives, out of your system?"

"Yes. I'm looking for something slightly more predictable."

"All right, then."

There was little in the way of conversation during the return flight—Dombrowski's snoring made sure of that. We arrived back in Nassau about lunch time. On docking, Gertie handed me a sealed envelope.

"I'd planned to leave this with you in Pensacola. For now, let's keep the arrangement business-only. You seem a little too rootless. I want to be sure you're ready to settle down before sharing my berth, as you call it. You can book a room at a hotel."

"All right. When do I start work?"

"Tomorrow will be soon enough. But you can come to the house for dinner tonight, if you'd like...."

"Yes, I would like."

I checked into the finest place in town. I was flush. Gertie had given me five hundred dollars. Added to the five hundred I was holding in escrow for Liz, and the three hundred of Aggie's, I had quite a little nest egg. What's more, my future seemed bright. After having dealt with that airborne harem of malcontented wives, keeping Gertie happy would be a snap. All I needed to do was convince her of my fidelity.

After lunch, I took a leisurely stroll about town and quickly concluded I needed a hat. The afternoon sun was relentless. I dropped in at what looked like a promising shop and the playful girl at the counter offered to help me select one. She teased and flattered, and flirted with me shamefully. Twice, she casually asked where I was staying. I merely smiled in return. Such was my resolve.

For the rest of the afternoon, every female I set eyes on looked stunningly attractive. It was as if they'd been called into service just to test my aforementioned resolve. Nevertheless, no matter how provocative the gait, short the skirt, or gay the smile, not one of them was able to turn my head. It took a thoroughly miserable-looking blonde wearing half-moon eyeglasses and a ponytail to do that. She was sitting on a shabby suitcase outside a steamship office.

"Eugenia? What are you doing here?"

"Oh, it's you." She smiled weakly. "I'm... I'm hoping to get on a boat to Tortuga."

"Tortuga?"

"Yes. I'm still looking for that friend of mine."

"Jack, you mean?"

"Well, actually it's someone else I'm looking for. I don't suppose you could spare..."

"Of course. Have you eaten?"

"No. Not since yesterday.... Things haven't gone as planned."

"They rarely do. Well, why don't we get you a room at my hotel? Then tomorrow, you can start out fresh."

"I'd really appreciate that. Do the rooms come with a bath?"

"Oh, yes. And the food's not bad either. Let me take your bag."

I booked a room for her at the desk, but it wouldn't be available until that evening. After devouring half a chicken, two potatoes, and a fruit salad for dessert, she asked to use my bath.

An hour later, she met me on the veranda—looking clean, but just as miserable. I ordered drinks, and after quaffing her wine, she brightened a little. With the second glass, she became talkative.

"I waited in that cooler for an hour. I was turning blue. So I crept out and found there was no one in the house."

"You didn't check the basement."

"The basement?"

"A sort of informal dungeon. They had me strapped to a fiendish device designed to lop off one's fingers in bite-sized bits."

"How horrible!"

She next related how she'd escaped Barataria on a rum-runner bound for Corpus Christi, and from there caught a tramp steamer stopping in Nassau. I also learned that the friend she was looking for was a woman named Giulia somebody. By the third glass, she'd revealed something more telling.

"I think she may be aboard an airship."

"A lot of them around."

"Yes. But this one is made up entirely of women. It's called *The Midnight Sun*."

"You're kidding."

"No, perfectly serious. Why?"

"Well, I've encountered that ship. In fact, I believe my would-be wife may be aboard it now."

"Would-be wife?"

"Fiancée. Well, former fiancée."

"Oh, sorry."

"No need. All water under the bridge now."

"Tell me, did you meet any others aboard it?"

"Well, a defector named Liz Rutledge, aka Antiope."

"Antiope?"

"Yes. Nice girl. Married my steamfitter."

"Oh. How about a tall woman with long black hair?"

"Does she have a loathing of men?"

"Oh, I wouldn't call it a loathing, exactly... let's say a strong dislike. Though she can be a little... tetchy."

"Yes, I've seen her in one of her tetchy moods. Calls herself Marpesia. She's the captain."

"Marpesia? Oh, no.... Tell me, she hasn't... killed anyone, has she?"

"Not in my presence. But I get the feeling she wouldn't be too upset at the thought."

Eugenia switched to martinis at that point, and after two of them, I was helping her upstairs. Her room still wasn't ready, so I let her have my bed.

"I'll check in on you later," I said at the door, then went out for a walk.

Though I'd given up hope of having any sort of reconciliation with Sesbania, I did want to see her again. If for no other reason than to make a clean break. Until meeting Eugenia, that seemed an impossibility. Chasing after *The Midnight Sun* and its Amazon crew just wasn't practical—nor would it be prudent. But what if I got them to come to me?

I happened to be waiting my turn in a barber shop as these thoughts occurred to me, absentmindedly flipping through an issue of *Rum-Runner's World*. The editorial content was all geared toward the particular concerns of that trade. But I surmised from the advertising its readership spanned both sides of the rum-runner–pirate divide. In the back there were classifieds: one section devoted to airships, new; one to airships, used; one to positions available (cutthroats predominating); and another to positions wanted (small-town clerks hoping to break into the profession). Most interesting, however, was the section devoted to ransom notices. This issue was some weeks old, and contained the notice Lafitte had placed for Clem:

One female, late of Desecheo. Age 28, chestnut hair, mole on bum (right cheek). Pleasant disposition, good teeth. Answers to Clematis. Wire funds to First Bank of Tortuga, attn: Charles Lavage, mgr. Just $5,000 if you act by Thursday next.... Then it's to the block with her! ^@^!

The odd combination of symbols at the end puzzled me. But the fellow sitting beside me explained it was the typographical equivalent of a cackle.

By the sheerest coincidence, the journal's office was just a few blocks from the barber's. On finishing, I went there and filled out the form:

One female, late of Byblos, NY. Age ca. 20, blonde hair, ponytail, half-moon eyeglasses. Suffers from literary allusions, but otherwise appears healthy. Answers to Eugenia. Open to offers, possible swap. Reply c/o this office, Box 371.

I hesitated before handing my slip to the clerk. Was

this the act of a man anticipating a predictable future? Probably not. But predictability, I reasoned, is something best eased into slowly.

I arrived at Gertie's promptly at seven. We had a lovely dinner. She waved off any talk of the future, instead telling me about her unprofitable childhood. It was one of those crushingly dull, blissful ones, offering no opportunity to blackmail either parent. Poor girl. I tried comforting her with some affectionate embracing out on her terrace, but she quite abruptly informed me she had work to attend to.

"I'll see you at nine tomorrow and we can figure out what you're good for."

I would have been happy to show her then, but that, regrettably, wasn't on the evening's docket. It certainly might have saved me a good bit of trouble later had she been a little flexible with her scheduling.

Back at the hotel, I rapped lightly on my door.

"Oh!" Eugenia replied, startled.

"It's me."

"Oh. Yes, of course."

She opened the door and looked at me curiously. I mean that in both senses. She eyed me in a way she'd never done previously. And her mouth hung partway open, as if she were about to speak but had forgotten what she was going to say.

I glanced down at my sole piece of luggage where it lay open on the bed. She'd been packing my things.

"I thought since I'd slept in your bed, I'd give you mine next door," she explained.

"Either way," I said, then noticed the vial I'd left on the dresser. It had been opened. Then she noticed me noticing it.

"Oh... I'm sorry.... Curiosity." She went over and re-placed the cap—but only after taking a long whiff.

It was devoid of perfume. But not, evidently, its lin-gering effect....

CHAPTER 11.

DIRTY LINEN

Discretion demands I withhold the details of that night. The girl had come upon the narcotic unwittingly and seemed ill prepared for its motivating properties—ill prepared, but not altogether ill disposed. She wasn't quite as aggressive as the others of my experience. But she *was* insistent.

When I awoke she was still fast asleep, and looking the very image of innocence. However committed she'd been to the evening's enterprise, I couldn't help but suspect there might be some feelings of regret once the drug ran its course. Some girls make a sport of dropping their inhibitions. And some, Eugenia Biddle among them, do not. I straightened up the bed as best I could without waking her, and then took my things into the next room.

Two hours later, she was tapping on my door asking if I wanted to breakfast on the veranda. As I expected, she made not the slightest allusion to her stirring performance. Quite the opposite.

"Sorry I was such a wet blanket last night. I was dead tired. I don't even remember you leaving the room."

From her expression, I gathered she was looking for some sort of reassurance.

"Oh, it wasn't five minutes after my arrival. You looked exhausted. Barely said a word."

Whether she actually believed that version or not, I can't say for certain. From her relieved expression, I'd guess she did. (Though you can be sure the chambermaid would not be so easily fooled.) The only truth in my account was the last bit. As a matter of fact, she hadn't spoken at all.

From then on, our conversation concerned Emmie.

"Remember how you told me your cousin claims to have written *The Circensiad*?" she asked.

"Not exactly. Only to have edited it heavily. See, she maintains that you sent her a trove of such things. Or maybe I should say, *will* send."

"How could it be both?"

"Well, that's where things get a little strange. Maybe this should wait until the cocktail hour?"

"None for me today, thanks. Besides, what could be stranger than what I've been through these last few weeks?"

"All right. Just remember, you insisted. Well, about twenty years back—1903, it was—Emmie claimed she was visited by an airship in Prospect Park."

"Prospect Park?"

"Near their apartment in Brooklyn. The airship dropped a crate full of manuscripts, letters, etc. What's more, this crate was addressed to her."

"How odd."

"I haven't gotten to the odd part yet. The principal item in this archive was a memoir. Yours."

"But I was just a baby in 1903!"

"Yes. In fact, not even born yet. The airship visitation came in February...."

"...And I was born in June. The whole thing's just ridiculous."

"Oh, it's that, all right. But I still haven't gotten to the most ridiculous part: you sent it from the year 1959."

She stared at me blankly. Pretty much anytime you

give someone a taste of Cousin Emmie you can expect a blank stare as reply. But being a party to Emmie's deliria must be particularly disorienting.

"Nineteen fifty-nine?" She drew each syllable out. "I don't get it."

"She claims you sent it from the future."

"But, even if that were possible, how would I even know about her?"

"She was a college chum of your mother's. Emmie Reese is her full name, née McGinnis."

"My mother never mentioned her."

"Well..." I couldn't very well tell the girl she was the daughter of Emmie's school chum's fictional equivalent. "I believe they had a falling out."

"Oh.... Still, why would I send this to her?"

"That's always been the fly in the ointment. In Emmie's version, you've caught wind of her literary fame and so wanted to avail yourself of her expertise."

"*Is* she famous?"

"No. But she says that could come at any time, perhaps even posthumously. There's a certain type of writer for whom hope doesn't merely spring eternal, it springs delusional. They can't stop themselves from writing and hoping."

"It's a condition. *Cacoëthes scribendi*, it's called. What did she do with these manuscripts?"

"Well, as with *The Circensiad*, she edits them to her satisfaction and then tries to get them published."

"Tries to?"

"She's been at it twenty years and so far hasn't found any takers."

"Sort of romantic, isn't it?"

"Not the word that usually comes to mind."

"How old is she?"

"How old? Late forties."

"Suppose she lives another twenty years and dies still seeking a publisher. Why, the story alone will get her books published."

"Yes, perhaps. But, of course, she'll be dead."

"But *I* won't. Nineteen fifty-nine, you said?"

"Yes."

She took out a little notebook and made a notation. Then asked for Emmie's address. "Her address in 1903, I mean."

I gave it to her. After jotting that down she stopped and stared ahead, musing.

"I have one more question. A very important question. How did I sign the manuscript?"

"Let me think…. Ah. Are you married now?"

"No… Oh, for God's sake, tell me!"

"Well, I'd forgotten until you mentioned it. But it was signed, Eugenia B. Tigue."

"Jack! Oh, my God."

Much to my surprise, she didn't seem to find the prospect to her liking. I tried to lessen the blow: "I suppose there are plenty of other Tigues out there."

"No. The Fates are once again toying with me."

"Bonnet's daughters? Have you met them?"

"What?"

"Ah, nothing really. Sorry."

With Eugenia's mind now elsewhere, I returned to my breakfast. What I found particularly ironic was that by relating Emmie's version of events, I—a skeptic—may have actually set them in motion. Now we both had something to think about.

But, regrettably, little time to do it in. I was just finishing a rather bland omelet when a fellow in uniform approached our table with a couple underlings covering my flanks.

"Mr. Van Slyke, I have come to arrest you."

It was the chief of police. I recognized him from the interrogation he'd attended during my first visit to Nassau.

"On what charge?"

"White slavery."

"I don't know what you're talking about."

"I'm not a white slave," Eugenia assured him.

"Do you deny placing an ad in the magazine *Rum-Runner's World*, offering a young woman named Eugenia for trade?"

From the look she gave me, I surmised Eugenia wouldn't be quite so free with the testimonials going forward.

"I can explain that...."

"Yes, of course you can. But you'll do it at the police station. Come. You too, young lady. I'll need a statement."

Things didn't go well at the station. I explained that having seen similar ads in the journal, I assumed it was all aboveboard. But by some convoluted reasoning, the Bahamians held that selling advertising to kidnappers wasn't a crime, whereas purchasing those ads was. The trick was to place the ad by mail. A subtle legal point that no doubt turned on the fact that the publisher of the journal was the brother-in-law of the chief of police.

At one point between interrogations, Eugenia and I were both waiting in the hallway and I had a chance to speak with her.

"I was going to tell you about it after breakfast. The

idea was to get your friend Marpesia to come to us. Nothing untoward was intended. You must believe me."

"I suppose that makes sense.... But what was that about suffering from literary delusions?"

"No, no. I quite clearly wrote literary *allusions*. Someone must have made a mistake transcribing it."

"But why 'suffers from'?"

Given the circumstances, it seemed an odd detail to fix on. But I was saved from having to answer when I was dragged down to the cells.

The jailers were considerate enough to remember my old room number, and I took some comfort in the familiarity of my surroundings—though not the stench. The cell's last occupant must have been afflicted with a digestive disorder.

Not long after I declined the midday plate of beans and rice, my lawyer showed up. It was the same shipping clerk who'd represented me so inadequately at my previous trial.

"No offense, but I'm planning to hire a real lawyer this time."

"You could, provided you had the money."

"I had over a thousand U.S. dollars when I was arrested."

"Yes, well, five hundred of that you stole from Miss Littko. And the suspicion is, you came upon the rest in the same way."

"That's ridiculous! Gertie herself can tell you!"

"It's Miss Littko who filed the charge."

"Then who sent you?"

"She did. Said it would be wrong to let them try and hang you without a lawyer. You're lucky she's such a forgivin' soul."

"Did you say 'try and hang' me?"

"We take white slavery very seriously here—*and* the right to a speedy trial."

Over the next week, I had no visitors save my so-called lawyer and my old friend, the night jailer. He came by about eleven every evening to cackle over old times.

Then came my trial. At least this time I was tried in a real court before a real judge. Not that it made much difference. The preponderance of evidence was incontrovertible. The newspapers declared it an open-and-shut case. Gertie didn't testify in person, but her affidavit was read in court. In it, she claimed I stole the money that evening after our arrival when I dined at her home.

The sole thing working in my favor was the teary-eyed testimony of Eugenia—if only she'd known when to stop. She held steadfast to the view that I was an upright fellow, even if, she told them, I'd offered to swap her for some other poor innocent held by pirates... and, back in Barataria, had placed her in cold storage.... (She concluded with an involuntary shiver, thus putting the final nail in my coffin.)

Wasting no time, the judge put on a little black cap. He'd just opened his mouth to speak, when Gertie's head henchman crept up to the bench and whispered in his ear.

The judge took off the black cap, muttering something about the coddling of society's detritus.

"Life at hard labor."

Well, not good—but better than the hangman's noose.

Why had Gertie lied about the five hundred dollars? I could only suppose she felt betrayed on hearing about Eugenia. Perhaps that nosy hotel maid was in her employ. Whether she was also behind the white slavery charge, I couldn't be sure. But it was certainly a mistake to have upset her. I tried sending a note through my so-called lawyer, but he brought it back unopened and smelling like something which had recently passed through a drunken gob's kidneys.

They left me to wonder about the hard labor for a few days. Then a fellow came and led me out into the sun.

"Just gots to fill some barrels. Nothin' to it."

"Doesn't sound difficult."

It wasn't until we rounded a corner and came upon Higgins' Hygienic Abattoir, Alfred Higgins, prop., that I began having second thoughts. Call it what you will, a slaughterhouse is still a slaughterhouse.

I can say one thing about the work, however: promotion came quick. By that very evening, I was made chief offal packer—the previous holder of the office having passed away a scant hour earlier....

~~~ *The End ...or is it?* ~~~

Those interested in how our hero escapes from this sad state of affairs will be happy to learn that the story continues....

No Time for Fish Tales, the third and final book of the Empyreal Privateer series, is available at all finer bookstores.

The piece that follows is Van Slyke's fascinating account of how he managed to gain an appointment to the United States Naval Academy at Annapolis.

THE ART OF THE FEEL

From the memoirs of E. Pluribus Van Slyke, Lt. (jg), Ret.

I'm told one ought to begin as Homer did, *in medias res,* which in this case means with my hand in her kimono. Her expression was perfect: nine parts surprise to one of offense, with only the merest hint of outrage. And my timing flawless—her girl, having been summoned by the electric bell, was just arriving with a fresh pot of coffee. As she opened the door, her mistress turned an open-mouthed gaze upon her and I withdrew my hand.

"Oh!" they harmonized.

"Coffee," the still-stupefied elocutionist added in a vague monotone while staring at the pot.

"The bell... I heard it ring...."

"Sorry, must have bumped into it," I confessed. "Got caught up in the excitement. Teddy's inaugural address." I held up the pamphlet I'd been reading aloud as proof. "Hot stuff!"

Biting her cheek, the girl exchanged the pot for the cold one on the sideboard and made her exit.

"I... I don't know what to say...," her mistress said.

"Just an accident. I was trying to gesticulate, the way you told me to. Barely grazed your kimono. Look, you don't think..."

"I'm not sure what to think. It was certainly more than barely grazing. And this isn't a kimono!"

She seemed more peeved about the nomenclature than the intrusion, and once I conceded the sartorial point, she calmed herself.

"Let us go on, but perhaps you could move to the center of the room. That will afford more room for your gestures."

I went back to reciting Teddy's speech and the incident was dropped. I don't know if she believed my explanation, but the fact is it would have taken a good deal of exploration below decks to actually get hold of anything worth the effort. This was, after all, 1911, and any woman entertaining outside of a brothel generally wore several layers of undergarments beneath her kimono—whatever she called it.

But the odds were she did believe it. I'd been lying since I could talk, and by the age of seventeen I'd gotten rather good at it, even if I do say so myself. Oh, plenty of people were on to me—most of my relations, and the brighter of my friends. And nearly all of my teachers. It would take them a few months, usually. Then one day they'd look me in the eye and smile. "What a little liar you are, Pluribus," they'd say, very pleased with themselves for having caught on. Of course, my Latin teacher was onto me by the second class. She didn't say a word. Just slipped on that sardonic grin of hers, while shaking her head ever so slowly—then finishing with one of her dismissive noises. I've known more than my share of such women, the ones who can mock with a half-formed syllable. But she was in a class by herself. This one was a nearly inaudible "ti," formed with the tongue stopping well short of the teeth.

When the lesson was over (elocution, not Latin), we made an appointment for the next week, and by pressing the button on the side of the desk I'd pretended to bump against earlier, she summoned the housemaid to show me out. As soon as we left the room, the girl stifled a giggle. I knew her, through her brother, so this bit of familiarity wasn't taking much of a liberty. I could have offered her the same explanation I'd given her mistress, but there was good reason to think she wouldn't have believed it. Besides, that would have been counter to my purpose.

"I hope we can trust you," I said. "To keep it to yourself."

"Well, everything comes at a price."

Her attitude was just as I'd hoped.

"Look, don't press her. Just be worse for me. Here."

I handed her five dollars. It disappeared into the folds of her skirt.

"He gives me ten."

She didn't need to tell me who *he* was.

"It's all I've got. Please, Dora."

We were at the front door by now.

"All right. Say hi to Jimmy."

She was smiling a sly, conspiratorial smile as she closed the door, and I took that as confirmation of a successful conclusion to this phase of the operation.

There are, to be sure, myriad ways of gaining an appointment to the Naval Academy at Annapolis. But this was my way and I'm damned proud of it. It was by no means a flawlessly executed campaign. My first sortie was a flop, and the second ended in ignominious defeat. In the end, it took all my Yankee ingenuity and pigheaded optimism to bring home the victory.

Looking back at it now, it isn't the *how* that strikes me so much as the *why*. There was a line of reasoning, of course. Sometime before my seventeenth birthday, when I discovered how thoroughly I enjoyed my Latin studies (lapped them up, one might say), I got it into my head that I should attend college. And I don't mean some state institution for turning out school teachers or well-rounded farmers, but an honest-to-God college, rich in tradition and alumni who could do me favors down the road.

The big fly in the ointment lay in the fact I was an orphan, left without a penny. I lived with a widowed aunt who'd had her savings crimped in a panic a few years before, 1907 I think it was. Her daughter, my cousin, seemed fairly flush, so I tried interesting her and her husband in the project. The problem there was that they were well acquainted with my character. I don't remember their precise words, but something along the lines of "fat chance." It was then my cousin's husband, an odd fellow whom I never quite figured out, suggested I make a play for one of the military academies.

"All expenses paid. And a uniform that makes women weak in the knees. Where could you do better than that?"

I only found out years later that he meant it as a joke. At the time, however, I took it as an inspired suggestion. Of course, having been exposed to the history of the war with Spain and the ensuing Philippine rebellion, I had a pretty clear idea of how rotten life could be in the army—living in swamps, eating from cans of rancid meat, fighting off ungrateful natives, and finally dying from any one of a variety of tropical fevers. The navy, meanwhile, spent its time sailing safely out at sea, or stopping in well-provisioned ports of call to show the flag and impress the native women with their smart uniforms. The one naval battle I knew anything about was Manila Bay, which took about as long as mixing a cocktail, and with the same level of danger.

So Annapolis it was. Never mind the only boats I'd had any experience with were canoes and primitive river ferries. There were plenty of appointees from out west who would have had less than that.

In time, I'd learn of several strong counter-arguments which I might have considered. For instance, the feverish way the upperclassmen have of hazing the new arrivals. Or the absurd strictures ruling life on board ship. Even on dry land, for that matter. And a little research would have brought to the fore any number of unpleasant predicaments experienced by seamen during times of war. An encyclopedia entry on Lord Nelson would have done the trick. But I was young, and when you are a pigheaded optimist of a certain age and an idea has planted itself in your mind, no matter how idiotic, it soon becomes all-consuming.

In those days, the entrance examination was a breeze for anyone who had attended an actual high school. But you still needed a sponsor. I knew on reaching my senior year that one of our members of Congress (House or Senate, I shan't say) had an appointment opening up, so it was just a matter of making my pitch. I led with the poor-orphan card. This could generally be counted on to soften up adults—useful in my case to mitigate the consequences of some peccadillo.

Not wanting to rely solely on the man's sympathy—for all I knew, he despised orphans—I simultaneously began to cultivate local politicians of the same party. As a rule, cultivating politicians is a pretty simple task—if you've got the stomach for it. All you need to do is tell them how clever they are. Then repeat it, ad nauseam. As luck would have it, the fellow I targeted was himself an able finagler so there was no need to lay it on that thick.

He knew what I was up to and probably liked me the better for it. At the time, he was just the local mayor, but he was well connected and highly ambitious. In fact, were I to mention his name, it would be instantly recognized.

So I had a two-pronged attack. On the one flank, the play for sympathy. On the other, good old-fashioned bootlicking. Seemed a sure thing. But in this case, it was no go. I was told the fellow with the appointment to hand out was a horse trader of the old school and knew precisely the value of his perks. Sold to a mill owner with a prodigal-son problem, the appointment could be worth a few thousand. Or it might be used to turn sentiment in some locale which voted badly in the last election. You know the sort of thing—bestowing the appointment on a favorite son with a stump speech sopping with patriotic blather.

Well, I had lost round one. But being pigheaded in my optimism, I wasn't the least bit discouraged. It just meant a little more exertion was needed to find the old boy's weak points. Here I came into some luck. It seemed the sister of a friend of mine worked as a housemaid in the home of my target in a city not too far away, the post being boodle her farmer father had earned for his loyalty to the party—in those days, party loyalty ran pretty cheap. Anyway, this friend, Jimmy, was rather proud of his tenuous connection to minor greatness. He was always sharing little bits of gossip his sister had picked up. The most useful was my mark's penchant for playing poker—and for real money.

I was something of a card player myself. Cheat, some might call me. But I came upon the talent honestly, via my aforementioned cousin, who was an able sharp herself. Queer woman—insane, most likely—and the object of my first crush, but that can wait for another time. Anyway, the point is I had this talent and profited by it. Mostly with boys my own age, but also, occasionally, with out-of-towners staying at the local hotels.

Being a pigheaded optimist, I concluded from this scant evidence that if I could get my mark into a serious game, I could thoroughly trounce him. And thus subdued, he'd be more than happy to swap the appointment for relief from his debt. It was, perhaps, the least-well-reasoned scheme in a long life of scheming, and I'm more than a little embarrassed by it.

By fleecing any of the locals foolish enough to enter a game with me, I built up a bankroll of a few hundred. Then, each Friday afternoon for three weeks running, I traveled to the city where the venerable member of Congress resided and checked into the plushiest hotel for the weekend. By tipping well, I was made privy to the high-stakes games in town.

It was on the night of my third Saturday that I finally found myself in a game with my mark. And it was then that I made my boner. I'd been doing admirably well on these weekend jaunts, even when playing fair, a novelty for me. So I started the game with a little more than thirteen hundred dollars. The question you're probably asking yourself is why didn't I just offer the old man the thirteen hundred as a straightforward, completely aboveboard bribe. It's one I've asked myself many times, believe me. Youthful arrogance is my only excuse.

Whether he would have taken it, who can say. What I can say is that the despicable old coot had that sixth sense for detecting a cheat which ruins so many otherwise pleasurable evenings. I'd held back for the first half-dozen hands, and even then attempted only the merest sort of infraction, the type of thing which can usually be explained away as an honest mistake. Not with this bastard. He had some cronies hanging about and suggested they show me out. After giving me a sound hiding, they threw me bodily into the alley at the rear of the hotel. I landed beside the stable, in one of those pools of brown liquid you often find beside stables, thoroughly ruining a fairly expensive suit. Yes, it was borrowed, but that was small comfort during the humiliating train ride home.

Well, even my pigheaded optimism had taken it on the chin. I spent the next week just licking my wounds and conjugating Latin. Strangely, I suppose, I'd come to find that a good restorative.

I began rethinking my plans. Given the success I'd had at the gaming tables—prior to being beaten and dumped in the alley—I wondered if attending one of the elite schools, say a Harvard or Yale, or, if not those, a Hamilton or Amherst, might not be within my means. After all, any of these would be sure to have plenty of plump victims ready for the plucking. But when I broached the subject with some of my teachers, I found little encouragement. My Latin mistress actually laughed, the only time I remember her going to the effort, the sardonic grin being so effective.

It was soon after this that Jimmy related how his sister, Dora, had left the service of the venerable member and was now working for an elocutionist on his recommendation.

"Kind of a step down, isn't it?" I asked.

"Yeah. Ma says she's out of her head. And Pa won't talk to her."

"Is this elocutionist a relation of the old man?"

"Dora says she's something like a niece. He takes lessons from her. Sees her a few times a week, whenever he's in town."

"Something like a niece?"

"Yeah. Real smart, Dora says. And pretty."

I didn't doubt that. For some reason it never occurred to Jimmy to wonder what use a sixty-year-old professional blowhard had for an elocutionist. And an attractive one, at that. But I was well acquainted with eccentricities in pedagogy.

My surmise also explained the transfer of Dora. The old man assumed it would be safer to have someone in the home of his mistress whom he felt he could trust. No doubt Dora was already privy to much she'd wisely not shared with her garrulous family. I'd found my mark's weakness.

As it happened, Dora was coming to town the next day to see her family, so I made a point of running into her. I told her about my collegiate plans and that my teachers had recommended I see an elocutionist to improve my patter. She promised to put forward my request. Two days later, I received a friendly note from the woman herself outlining terms. Five dollars a session. Pretty dear, since presumably all mine would include was the tutelage in elocution. Nonetheless, I accepted and the next Saturday ventured to her home— a large, well-appointed flat in one of the finer buildings in that city.

She greeted me in a kimono, her favored attire when giving lessons. Strictly speaking, it wasn't a kimono, but a sort of housedress in that style. But definitely no corset, or need for one. Everything was right where it ought to be. She was a tall woman, but not awkwardly so. Statuesque, I suppose. And the epitome of poised.

In the course of our time together, I made some vague hints at other avenues of approach, some fairly suggestive—for the time, anyway—but she either ignored them or batted them down with an unflattering finality. From that, I concluded that she actually was an elocutionist, and whatever went on with the venerable member was just a lucrative sideline.

Before leaving, I learned just how lucrative. She received a phone call, and from the tone and content, I deduced it was the man in question. She said nothing to give away his identity, but made several playful remarks. And talked of a gift she had coming. By the time she hung up, one thing had been made crystal clear—she called the tunes.

I returned home and considered my next move. The obvious course was to simply blackmail the old goat into giving me the appointment or risk my revealing his mistress. But I rejected that out of hand. Not that I have any qualms about extortion. Far from it. I was blackmailing my own father from the time I was seven and caught him in the orchard with a neighbor's wife.

But my father was a spare-the-rod type. And from the speed and manner with which he'd had me ejected from the hotel, I concluded that the venerable member was decidedly not—and I wasn't willing to risk life as a cripple to find out just how far he'd go. Besides, there was a good chance the local journalists, aldermen, etc.— even his own wife—were already in on the secret.

No, something more subtle was required. How exactly I came upon the ingenious scheme I can't say. A stroke of luck, certainly. But luck favors the diligent, in scheming just as in life generally. And no boy ever put more effort into scheming than I did. Tom Sawyer was a layabout by comparison.

The plan was based on this simple premise: if his beguiling mistress put it into his head to appoint a certain young scamp to the Naval Academy, *and* made it clear her affection was riding on it, the old man would likely welcome the notion as a less expensive alternative to the Tiffany bracelet I'd heard mentioned over the telephone.

But how to persuade the woman to plead my case? What I needed was something with which to blackmail *her*. Something she couldn't afford for her paramour to find out. For instance, if she were carrying on with some other man. At my next lesson, I brought Dora a small gift and tried wheedling some intelligence from her. She acknowledged the relationship with the venerable member, but swore there was no other. Then she drew a conclusion which I hadn't anticipated. She assumed the reason for my inquiry was that I myself was going to make a play for the lady's affection.

Seizing the moment, I confirmed that was my objective. And I went further. I led her to believe I'd received some encouragement. Later that day, as she was escorting me out after my lesson, I gave Dora a wink.

"You're kidding.... Really?" she whispered.

I merely smiled.

It was the following week the encounter occurred with which I opened this account. A week after that, I made a full confession to the elocutionist, first telling her about my craving for the appointment to Annapolis, and my orphan state.... I sensed from her mien, however, I hadn't touched her heart. Then she drove home the point.

"Are you trying to use me, you little scalawag?"

"Yes, I'm afraid I am. But if that rubs you the wrong way, you really won't like the alternative."

"What alternative?"

I then recounted my conversations with Dora, and the bribes. And reminded her of the scene with my hand in her kimono. And that the likely reason the old man had placed the girl there was so she could spy.

"What do you think would happen if today I were to snub the girl? Tell her she won't be getting another cent from me?"

Well, as you might guess, I hadn't risen any in the elocutionist's esteem. The torrid string of epithets she let loose lacked the careful delivery she espoused in her lessons, but was nonetheless plenty eloquent.

Still, she came around. They almost always do. She even complimented my resourcefulness, in a backhanded sort of way.

"I'll bet you end up in politics."

She was wrong about that, at least as far as holding office is concerned. I've gone low, but never that low. Besides, I've learned that staying out of the public eye is generally safer for an inveterate scalawag. My few brushes with notoriety have taught me that. There's always someone trying to knock the bigwig down, catch him with his hand in the public's pocket, or put him out in the next election. And tastes are fickle.

But there's always a demand for an unprincipled scamp....